"I suppose ther___ ___ ___ of...explanation?___

Loukas looked at her unhelpfully. "To what, Jess?"

"To you sitting here and behaving as if—"

That half smile again. "As if I own the place?"

She swallowed, thinking how arrogant he sounded. "Well, yes."

"Because I do own it," he said, suddenly impatient. "I've bought the company, Jess. I now own every one of the *Lulu* outlets, in cities and airports and cruise ships all over the world."

Shock rippled over her skin. *Stay focused*, she told herself. She kept her voice casual. "I didn't realize—"

"That I was rich enough?"

"Well, there's that of course." Her smile felt as if it was slicing her face in two. "Or that you had an interest in jewelry and watches."

Loukas touched the tips of his fingers together and stared into eyes which were the exact color of aquamarines. Jessica Cartwright. The one woman he'd never been able to forget. The woman who had unraveled him and then tied him up in knots. His pale and unexpected nemesis. He expelled a slow breath and let his gaze travel over her at a leisurely pace—because surely he had earned the right to study her as he would any other thing of beauty which he'd just purchased.

"There's plenty you don't know about me." His mouth hardened and he felt the delicious rush of blood to his groin. *And plenty she was about to find out.*

Sharon Kendrick once won a national writing competition describing her ideal date: being flown to an exotic island by a gorgeous and powerful man. Little did she realize that she'd just wandered into her dream job! Today she writes for Harlequin, featuring her often stubborn but always *to-die-for* heroes and the women who bring them to their knees. She believes that the best books are those you never want to end. Just like life...

Books by Sharon Kendrick

Harlequin Presents

Christmas in Da Conti's Bed
The Greek's Marriage Bargain
A Scandal, a Secret, a Baby
The Sheikh's Undoing
Monarch of the Sands
Too Proud to Be Bought

One Night With Consequences
Carrying the Greek's Heir

At His Service
The Housekeeper's Awakening

Desert Men of Qurhah
Defiant in the Desert
Shamed in the Sands
Seduced by the Sultan

Scandal in the Spotlight
Back in the Headlines

Visit the Author Profile page
at Harlequin.com for more titles.

Sharon Kendrick

The Ruthless Greek's Return

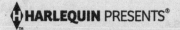

ISBN-13: 978-0-373-13831-9

The Ruthless Greek's Return

First North American publication 2015

Copyright © 2015 by Sharon Kendrick

Recycling programs for this product may not exist in your area.

HARLEQUIN®
www.Harlequin.com

Printed in U.S.A.

The Ruthless Greek's Return

This book acknowledges with grateful thanks
the help and inspiration given to me
by Piero Campomarte,
patron of the Citera Hotel in Venice.

Thanks also to one of the Citera's most famous
and favored guests—Dennis Riddiford.

CHAPTER ONE

Something was different. Jessica felt it the moment she walked into the building. An unmistakable air of excitement and expectation. A rippling sense of change. She felt her throat constrict with something which felt like fear. Because people didn't like change. Even though it was about the only thing in life you could guarantee, nobody really welcomed it—and she was right up there with all those change-haters, wasn't she?

Outwardly the headquarters of the upmarket chain of jewellery stores was the same. Same plush sofas and scented candles and twinkling chandeliers. Same posters of glittering jewels spilled casually onto folds of dark velvet. There were glossy shots of women gazing dreamily at engagement rings, while their impossibly handsome fiancés looked on. There was even a poster of *her*, leaning reflectively against a sea wall and gazing into the distance, with a chunky platinum watch gleaming against her wrist. Briefly, Jessica's gaze flicked over it. Anyone looking at that poster would think the woman in the crisp shirt and sleek ponytail inhabited a life which was all neat and sorted. She gave a wry smile. Whoever said the camera never lied had been very misguided.

Glancing down at her pale leather boots, which had somehow survived the journey from Cornwall without being splashed, she walked over to the desk where the receptionist was wearing a new blouse which displayed her ample cleavage. Jessica blinked. She was *sure* she could smell furniture polish mingling with the scent of gardenia from the flickering candles. Even the extra-large display of roses sitting on the fancy glass desk looked as if they'd been given a makeover.

'Hi, Suzy,' said Jessica, bending her head to sniff at one of the roses and finding it completely without fragrance. 'I have a three o'clock appointment.'

Suzy glanced down at her computer screen and smiled. 'So you do. Nice to see you, Jessica.'

'Nice to be here,' said Jessica, although that bit wasn't *quite* true. Her life in the country had claimed her wholesale and she only came to London when she had to. And today it seemed she had to—summoned by an enigmatic email, which had provoked more questions than it had answered and left her feeling slightly confused. Which was why she had abandoned her jeans and sweater and was standing in reception in her city clothes, with the cool smile expected of her. And if inside her heart was aching because Hannah had gone…well, she would soon learn to deal with that. She had dealt with plenty worse.

Brushing fine droplets of water from her raincoat, she lowered her voice. 'You don't happen to know what's going on?' she said. 'Why I received a mystery summons out of the blue, when I'm not due to start shooting the new catalogue until early summer?'

Suzy started looking from side to side, like someone who had been watching too many spy films. 'Actually, I do.' She paused. 'We have a new boss.'

Jessica's smile didn't slip. 'Really? First I've heard about it.'

'Oh, you wouldn't have heard anything.

Big takeover deal—very hush-hush. The new owner's Greek. Very Greek. A playboy by all accounts,' said Suzy succinctly, her eyes suddenly darkening. 'And *very* dangerous.'

Jessica felt the hairs on the back of her neck prickle, as if someone had just stroked an icy finger over her skin. Hearing someone say *Greek* shouldn't produce a reaction, but the stupid thing was that it did, every time. It wasn't as bad as it used to be, but she could never hear the mention of anything Hellenic without the sudden rush of blood to her heart. She was like one of Pavlov's dogs, who used to salivate whenever a bell was rung. One of those dumb dogs who expected to be fed and instead were presented with nothing but an empty bowl. And how sad was that? She stared at Suzy and injected a light-hearted note into her voice.

'Really?' she questioned. 'You mean dangerous as in swashbuckling?'

Suzy shook her mop of red curls. 'I mean dangerous as in oozing sex appeal, and knows it.' A light flashed on her desk and she clicked the button with a perfectly manicured fingernail. 'Something which you're just about to find out for yourself.'

Jessica thought about Suzy's words as she rode in the elevator towards the penthouse offices, wishing they could have swopped places. Because the new boss would be completely wasted on her—no matter how hunky he was. She'd met men who'd oozed testosterone and she'd had her fingers burnt. She stared at her reflection in the smoky elevator mirrors. Actually, it had only been one man and she'd had her whole body burnt—her heart and soul completely fried—and as a consequence she steered clear of *dangerous* men and all the stuff which came with them.

The elevator stopped and the first thing Jessica noticed was that things were different up here, too. More flowers, but the place was deserted and oddly quiet. She'd expected a small delegation of executives or some sort of fanfare, but even the usual rather scary-looking assistant who guarded the inner sanctum was missing. She looked around. The doors to the executive suite were open. She glanced down at her watch. Dead on three. So did she just walk in and announce herself? Or hang around here and wait until someone came out to find her? For a moment she stood there feeling slightly uncertain, when a richly accented voice brushed over her skin like gravel which had been steeped in honey.

'Don't just stand there, Jess. Come right in. I've been waiting for you.'

Her heart clenched and at first she thought her mind was playing tricks. She told herself that all Mediterranean voices sounded similar and that it couldn't possibly be him. Because how could she instantly recognise a voice she hadn't heard for years?

But she was wrong. *Wrong, wrong, wrong.*

She walked into the office in the direction of the voice and stopped dead in the centre of the vast room. And even though her brain was sending out frantic and confused messages to her suddenly tightening body, there was no denying the identity of the man behind the desk.

It *was* him.

Loukas Sarantos, framed by the backdrop of a London skyline—looking like the king of all he surveyed. Big, and brooding and in total command. A mocking half-smile curved his lips. His long legs were spread out beneath the desk while his hands were spreadeagled on the expansive surface, as if emphasising that it all belonged to him. With a shock she noted the expensive charcoal suit which hugged his powerful frame and more confusion washed over her. Because Loukas was a bodyguard. A top-notch bodyguard with clothes which made him blend in, not stand out. What was he doing *here*, dressed like that?

He had been forbidden to her from the start and it was easy to see why. He could intimidate people with a single glance from those searing black eyes. He was like no one else she'd ever met, nor was ever likely to. He made her want things she hadn't even realised she wanted—and when he'd given them to her, he'd made her want even more. He was trouble. He was the night to her day. She knew that.

The room seemed to shift in and out of focus, blurring at the edges before reappearing with a clarity so sharp that it almost hurt her eyes. She wanted the sight of him to leave her cold. For him to be nothing but a distant reminder of another time and another life.

Some hope.

He was leaning back in a black leather chair, which gleamed like the thick hair that curled against his neck. But his half-smile held no trace of humour—it was nothing but an icy assessment which seemed to hit her like a chill wind. His eyes bored through her and for a moment Jessica felt as if she was going to faint, and part of her wondered if that might not be a good thing. Because if she crumpled to the floor, wouldn't that give her a let-out clause? Wouldn't it force him to ring for medical assistance, so that his potency would be diluted by the presence of other people?

But the feeling quickly passed and a lifetime of hiding her emotions meant she was able to look around the room with nothing but curiosity on her face and say almost casually, 'Where's the assistant who's usually here?'

A flicker of irritation passed across his face as he leaned forward. 'Eight years,' he said softly. 'Eight long years since we've seen each other—and all you can do is ask me some banal question about a member of staff?'

His confidence unnerved her almost as much as his appearance, because the brashness of yesteryear seemed to have disappeared—along with the beaten-up leather jacket and faded jeans. Yet even in his made-to-measure suit, he still exuded a carnal sexuality which nothing could disguise. Was that why the almost forgotten aching had started deep inside her? Why she suddenly found herself remembering the burn of his lips pressing down on hers and the impatience of his fingers as he pushed up her little tennis skirt and…and…

'What are you doing here?' she questioned, only suddenly she didn't sound quite so calm and she wondered if he'd picked up on that.

'Why don't you take off your coat and sit down, Jess?' he suggested silkily. 'Your face has gone very white.'

She wanted to tell him that she'd stay standing, but the shock of seeing him again really *had* affected her equilibrium. And maybe fainting wasn't such a good idea after all. She would only find herself horizontal—and imagine just how disconcerting it would be to find Loukas bending over her. Bending over her as if he wanted to kiss her…when the reality was that he was looking at her as if she'd recently crawled out from beneath a stone.

She walked over to the chair he'd indicated and sank down, letting her leather bag slide noiselessly to the ground as she lifted her gaze towards the empty blackness of his. 'This is a…surprise,' she said lightly.

'I imagine it must be. Tell me…' his eyes gleamed '…how it felt to walk into the room and realise it was me?'

She lifted her shoulders as if there were no

words to answer that particular question, and even if there were she wasn't sure she'd want him to hear them. 'I suppose there must be some sort of…explanation?'

He looked at her unhelpfully. 'To what, Jess? Perhaps you could be a little more specific.'

'To you sitting here and behaving as if—'

That half-smile again. 'As if I own the place?'

She swallowed, thinking how arrogant he sounded. 'Well, yes.'

'Because I do own it,' he said, suddenly impatient. 'I've bought the company, Jess—I should have thought that much was obvious. I now own every one of the Lulu outlets, in cities and airports and cruise ships all over the world.'

Shock rippled over her skin. Stay focused, she told herself. You can do it. You were trained in the art of staying focused.

She kept her voice casual. 'I didn't realise—'

'That I was rich enough?'

'Well, there's that, of course.' Her smile felt as if it were slicing her face in two. 'Or that you had an interest in jewellery and watches.'

Loukas touched the tips of his fingers together and stared into eyes which were the exact colour of aquamarines. As always, not a single strand of her blonde hair was out of place and he remembered that even after the most strenuous sex, it always seemed to fall back into a neat and shiny curtain. He looked at the pink gleam of her lips and something dark and nebulous whispered over his skin. Jessica Cartwright. The one woman he'd never been able to forget. The woman who had unravelled him and then tied him up in knots. His pale and unexpected nemesis. He expelled a slow breath and let his gaze travel over her at a leisurely pace—because surely he had earned the right to study her as he would any other thing of beauty which he'd just purchased.

As usual, her style was understated. Classy and cool. A streamlined body, which left the observer in no doubt about her athletic background. She'd never been into revealing clothes or heavy make-up—her look had always been scrubbed and fairly natural and that hadn't changed. He had been attracted to her in a way which had taken him by surprise and he'd never been able to work out why. He noticed how her white shirt hugged those neat little breasts and the subtle gleam of pearls at her ears. With her pale hair pulled back in a ponytail, which emphasised her high cheekbones, he thought how remote she seemed. How *untouchable*. And it was all a lie. Because behind the false ice-maiden image, wasn't there a woman as shallow and as grasping as all the others? Someone who would take what they wanted from you and then just leave you— gasping like a fish which had been tossed from the water.

'There's plenty you don't know about me.' His mouth hardened and he felt the delicious rush of blood to his groin. *And plenty she was about to find out.*

'I don't understand…' She shrugged her shoulders and now her aquamarine eyes were wide with question. 'The last time I saw you, you were a bodyguard. You worked for that Russian oligarch.' She frowned as if she was trying to remember. 'Dimitri Makarov. That was his name, wasn't it?'

'*Neh*. That was his name.' Loukas nodded. 'I was the guy with the gun inside his jacket. The guy who knew no fear. The wall of muscle who could smash through a plank with a single blow.' He paused and flicked her a look because he remembered the way she used to run those long fingers over the hard bulge of his muscles, cooing her satisfaction as she touched his iron-hard flesh. 'But one day I decided to start using my brains instead of just my brawn. I realised that a life spent protecting others has a very limited timescale and that I needed to look towards the future. And, of course, some women consider such men to be little more than *savages*—don't they, Jess?'

She flinched. He could see the whitening of her knuckles in her lap and her reaction gave him a rush of pleasure. Because he wanted to see her react. He wanted to see her coolness melt and to watch her squirm.

'You know I never said that.' Her voice was trembling.

'No,' he agreed grimly. 'But your father said it and you just stood there and agreed with every damned word, didn't you, Jess? You were complicit in your silence. The little princess, agreeing with Daddy. Shall I remind you of some of the other things he said?'

'No!' Her hand had flown to her neck, as if her fingers could disguise the little pulse which was working frantically there.

'He called me a thug. He said I would drag you down to the gutter where I came from, if you stayed with me. Do you remember that, Jess?'

She shook her head. 'Wh—why are we sitting here talking about the past?' she questioned and suddenly her voice didn't sound so cool. 'I dated you when I was a teenager and, yes, my father reacted badly when he found out we were…'

'Lovers,' he put in silkily.

She swallowed. 'Lovers,' she repeated, as if it hurt her to say it. 'But it all happened such a long time ago and none of it matters any more. I've…well, I've moved on and I expect you have, too.'

Loukas might have laughed if he hadn't felt the cold twist of rage. She had humiliated him as no woman had ever dared try. She had trampled on his foolish dreams—and she thought that none of it mattered? Well, he was about to show her that it did. That if you betrayed someone then sooner or later it would come back to haunt you.

He picked up a gold pen which was lying on his desk and began to twirl it between his thumb and forefinger, his eyes never leaving her face.

'Maybe you're right,' he said. 'It isn't the past we should be concentrating on, but the present. And, of course, the future. Or rather more importantly—your future.'

He saw her shoulders stiffen. Did she guess what was coming? Surely she realised that anyone in his position would set about terminating her contract with as little fallout as possible.

'What about it?'

He heard the defensiveness in her voice as he twirled the pen in the opposite direction. 'You've been working for the company for—how long is it now, Jess?'

'I'm sure you know exactly how long it is.'

'You're right. I do. I have your contract here in front of me.' He glanced down at it before looking up again. 'You joined Lulu right after you gave up your tennis career, yes?'

Jessica didn't answer straight away because she was afraid of giving herself away. She didn't want to show anything which might make her vulnerable to this very intimidating Loukas. Given up her tennis career? He made it sound as if she'd given up taking sugar in her coffee! As if the thing she'd devoted her entire life to—the sport she'd lived and breathed since she was barely out of nappies—hadn't suddenly been snatched away from her. It had left a great, gaping hole in her life and, coming straight after her break-up with him, it had been a double whammy she'd found difficult to claw her way back from. But she'd done it because it had been either sink or swim, and very soon after that she'd had Hannah to care for. So sinking had never really been an option. 'That's right,' she said.

'So why don't you tell me how you got the job, which I understand surprised a lot of people in the industry, since you had zero modelling experience?' He raised his eyebrows. 'Did you sleep with the boss?'

'Don't be stupid,' she snapped, before she could stop herself. 'He was a man in his sixties.'

'Otherwise you might have been tempted?' He leaned back in his chair and smiled, as if he was pleased to have got some kind of reaction from her at last. 'I know from my own experience that sportswomen have particularly *voracious* sexual appetites. You in particular were pretty spectacular in bed, Jess. And out of it. You could never get enough of me, could you?'

Jessica willed herself not to respond to the taunt, even though it was true. She felt as if he was toying with her, the way a cat sometimes toyed with a dragonfly just before its sheathed paw finally stilled the chattering wings. But for the time being she would play along. What choice did she have when the balance of power was so unevenly divided? Flouncing out of here wasn't an option, because this wasn't just about survival—it was about pride. She might have got the job by chance, but she'd grown into the unexpected career which fate had provided by way of compensation for her shattered dreams. She was *proud* of what she'd achieved and she wasn't going to toss it all away in a heated moment of retaliation, just because the man asking the questions was the man she'd never been able to forget.

'Do you want an answer to your question?' she asked quietly. 'Or are you just going to sit there insulting me?'

A hint of a smile tugged at the edges of his lips, but just as quickly it was gone. 'Carry on,' he said.

She drew in a deep breath, like one which used to fire her up just before she began a service game. 'You know I tore a ligament, which effectively ended my career?' She stared into his face, but any sympathy she might have been hoping for was absent. His cursory nod was an acknowledgment, not a condolence. There was no understanding in the cold gleam of his eyes. She wondered if he knew that her father had died.

'I heard you pulled out on the eve of a big tournament,' he said.

'I did.' She nodded. 'Obviously, there was a lot of publicity. I was…'

'You were poised on the brink of international success,' he interjected softly. 'Expected to win at least one Grand Slam, despite your precocious age.'

'That's right,' she said, and this time no amount of training could keep the faint crack of emotion from her voice. Didn't matter how many times she told herself that worse things had happened to people than having to pull out of a career before it had really begun—it still hurt. She thought of all the pain and practice. Of the friends and relationships she'd lost along the way. Of the disapproving silences at home and the way her father had pushed her and pushed her until she'd felt she couldn't be pushed any more. The endless sacrifices and the sense that she was never quite good enough. All ended with the sickening snap of her ligament as she ran across the court for a ball she was never going to reach.

She swallowed. 'The papers ran a photo of me leaving the press conference after I'd been discharged from hospital.' It had become an iconic image, which had been splashed all over the tabloids. Her face had been pale and edged with strain. Her trademark blonde plait falling over the narrow shoulders on which a nation's hopes had been resting.

'And?'

His bullet-like interjection snapped Jessica back to the present and she looked into the rugged beauty of his olive-skinned face. And wasn't it a mark of her own weakness that she found herself aching to touch it again? To whisper her fingertips all over its hard angles and hollows and feel the shadowed roughness of his jaw. Couldn't he blot out the uncomfortable way she was feeling with the power of one of his incredible kisses and make everything seem all right? She swallowed as she met the answering gleam in his eyes. As if he had guessed what she was thinking. And that was a mistake. It was the most important lesson drummed into her since childhood, that she could never afford to show weakness, not to anyone—but especially not to Loukas. Because hadn't he been trained to leap on any such weakness, and exploit it?

'Lulu noticed in the photo that I was wearing a plastic wristwatch,' she continued. 'And it just so happened that they were launching a sporty new watch aimed at teenagers and thought I had the ideal image to front their advertising campaign.'

'Yet you are not conventionally beautiful,' he observed.

She met the dark ice of his gaze, determined not to show her hurt, but you couldn't really blame someone for telling the truth, could you? 'I know I'm not. But I'm photogenic. I have that curious alchemy of high cheekbones and widely spaced eyes, which makes the camera like me—at least, that's what the photographer told me. I realised a long time ago that I look better in photos than in real life. That's why they took me on. I think they were just capitalising on all the publicity of my stalled career to begin with, but the campaign was a surprise success. And then when my father and stepmother were killed in the avalanche, I think they felt sorry for me—and of course, there was more publicity, which was good for the brand.'

'I'm sorry about your father and stepmother,' he said, almost as an afterthought. 'But these things happen.'

'Yes, I know they do.' She looked into his hard eyes and it was difficult not to feel defensive. 'But they wouldn't have kept me on all these years unless I was helping the watches to sell. That's why they keep renewing my contract.'

'But they aren't selling any more, because you are no longer a teenager,' he said slowly. 'And you no longer represent that age group.'

She felt a beat of disquiet. She told herself to forget they'd been lovers and to forget that it had ended so badly. She needed to treat him the way she would any other executive—male *or* female. Be nice to him. He's your sponsor. *Charm him.* 'I'm twenty-six, Loukas. That's hardly over the hill,' she said, managing to produce a smile from somewhere. The kind of smile a woman might use on a passing car mechanic, if she discovered her car had developed a puncture on a badly lit road. 'Even in these youth-obsessed times.'

She saw the flicker of a nerve at his temple

—as if he was aware of her charm offensive. As if he didn't approve of it very much. She wondered if she came over as manipulative but suddenly she didn't care, because she was fighting for her livelihood. And Hannah's, too.

'I don't think you understand what I'm saying, Jess.'

Jessica felt her future flash before her as it suddenly occurred to her why she was here. Why she'd received that terse email demanding her presence. Of *course* he had her contract on his desk. He now owned the company and could do anything he pleased. He was about to tell her that her contract wouldn't be renewed—that it only operated on a year-to-year basis. And then what would she do—a burntout tennis player with no real qualifications? She thought about Hannah and her college fees. About the little house she'd bought after she'd paid off all her father's debts. The house that had become their only security. About all the difficulties and heartbreak along the way, and the slow breaking down of barriers to arrive at the workable and loving relationship she had with her half-sister today.

A shiver whispered its way down her spine and she prayed Loukas wouldn't notice—even though he'd been trained to notice every little thing about other people. Especially their weaknesses.

'How can I understand what you're saying when you've been nothing but enigmatic?' she said. 'When you've sat there for the entire time with that judgemental look on your face?'

'Then perhaps I should be a little clearer.' He drummed his fingertips on the contract. 'If you want your contract extended, you might want to rethink your attitude. Being a little nicer to the boss might be a good place to start.'

'Be nice to you?' she questioned. 'That's rich. You're the one who has been hostile from the moment I walked into this office—and you still haven't told me anything.' There was a pause. 'What are you planning to do?'

Loukas swivelled his chair round, removing the distraction of her fine-boned face from his line of vision and replacing it with the gleam of the London skyline. It was a view which carried an eye-watering price tag. The view which reinforced just how far he had come. The space-age circle of the Eye framing the pewter ribbon of the river. Jostling for position among all the centuries-old monuments were all the new kids on the block—the skyscrapers aimed at the stars. A bit like him, really. He stared at the Walkie-Talkie building with its fabled sky garden. Whoever would have thought that the boy who'd once had to ferret for food at the back of restaurants would have ended up sitting here, with such unbelievable wealth at his fingertips?

It had been his burning ambition to crawl out of the poverty and despair which had defined his childhood. To make right a life steeped in bitterness and betrayal. And he had done as he had set out to, ticking off every ambition along the way. He'd done his best for his mother, even though... Painfully, he closed his eyes and refocused his thoughts. He'd made the fortune he'd always lusted after when he'd worked as a bodyguard for oligarchs and billionaires and seen their lavish displays of wealth. He'd always wondered what it would be like to carelessly lose a million dollars at a casino table and not even notice the loss. And he'd discovered that he used to get more pleasure from the food he'd been forced to steal from the restaurant bins when his belly was empty. Because that was the thing about money. The pleasure it was supposed to give you was a myth, peddled by those who were in possession of it. It brought nothing but problems and expectations. It made people behave in ways which sickened him.

Even when he'd been poor he'd never had a problem finding women, but he'd often wondered whether it would make a difference if you were rich. His mouth hardened. And it did. Oh, it did. He felt the acrid taste of old-fashioned disapproval in his mouth as he recalled the variety of *extras* women had offered him since he'd become a billionaire in his own right. Did he like to watch? Did he want threesomes? Foursomes? Was he interested in dressing up and role play? It had been made clear to him that anything he wanted was his for the taking and all he had to do was ask. And he had tried it all. He would have tried anything to fill the dark emptiness inside him, but nothing ever did. He'd cavorted with women with plastic bodies and gorgeous, vacuous faces. Models and princesses were his for the taking. So many things had been dangled in front of him in order to entice him, but he had been like a child let loose in a candy store who, after a few days of indulging himself, had felt completely jaded.

And that was when he had decided that you couldn't move on until your life was straightened out. Until you'd tied up all the loose ends which had threatened to trip you up over the years. His mother was dead. His brother was found. Briefly, he closed his eyes as he thought about the rest of that story and felt a painful beat of his heart. Which left only Jessica Cartwright. His mouth hardened. And she was a loose end he was going to take particular pleasure tying up.

He turned his chair back around. She was still sitting there, trying to hide her natural anxiety, and he allowed himself a moment of pure, sadistic pleasure. Because he wouldn't have been human if he hadn't appreciated the exquisite irony of seeing how much the tables had turned. How the snooty tennis prodigy who'd kept him hidden away like a guilty secret—while he *serviced her physical needs*—was now waiting for an answer on which her whole future would be decided.

How far would she go to keep her job? he wondered idly. If he ordered her to crawl under the desk and unzip him and take him in her mouth—would she oblige? He felt the hard throb at his groin as he imagined his seed spilling inside her mouth, before changing his mind. No. He didn't want Jess behaving like a hooker. What he wanted—what he *really* wanted—was for her to be compliant and willing and giving. He wanted her beneath him, preferably naked. He wanted to see her eyes darken and hear her gasp of disbelieving pleasure as he entered her. He wanted to feed her hunger for him, until she was dependent on him. Until she couldn't draw a breath without thinking of him.

And then he would walk away, just as she'd done.

The tables would be turned.

They would be equals.

He looked into her aquamarine eyes.

'You're going to have to change,' he said.

CHAPTER TWO

JESSICA'S HEART WAS pounding loudly as she looked across the desk at Loukas, who in that moment seemed to symbolise everything which was darkness...and power. As if he held her future in the palm of his hand and was just about to crush it.

He had begun removing the jacket of his beautiful suit. Sliding it from his shoulders and looping it over the back of his chair and that was making her feel even more disorientated. He looked so...intimidating. Yet the instant he started rolling up his sleeves to display his hair-roughened arms, it seemed much more like the Loukas of old. Sexy and sleek and completely compelling. Her thoughts were skittering all over the place and suddenly she was having to try very hard to keep the anxiety from her voice. 'What do you mean—I have to change? Change what, exactly?'

His smile didn't meet his eyes. In fact, it barely touched his lips. He was enjoying this, she realised. He was enjoying it a lot.

'Everything,' he said. 'But mostly, your image.'

Jessica looked at him in confusion. 'My image?'

Again, he did that thing of joining the tips of his fingers together and she was reminded of a head teacher who'd sent for an unruly pupil and was just about to give them a stern telling-off.

'I can't believe that nobody has looked at your particular advertising campaign before,' he continued. 'Or why it has been allowed to continue.' His black eyes glittered. 'A variation of the same old thing—year in and year out. The agency the company have been using have become complacent, which is why the first thing I did when I took over was to sack them.'

'You've sacked them?' Jessica echoed, her heart sinking—because she liked the agency they used and the photographer they employed. She only saw them once a year when they shot the Lulu catalogue but she'd got to know them and they felt *comfortable*.

'Profits have been sliding for the past two

years,' he continued remorselessly. 'Which isn't necessarily a bad thing—because it meant I was able to hammer out an excellent price for my buyout. But it does mean that things are going to be very different from now on.'

She heard the dark note in his voice and told herself to stay calm and find the strength to face her fears. Like when you were playing tennis against a tough opponent—it was no good holding back and being defensive and allowing them to dominate and control. You had to take your courage in your hands and rush the net. Face them head-on. She met his cold, black eyes.

'Is this your way of telling me that you're firing me?'

He gave a soft laugh. 'Oh, believe me, Jess—if I was planning on firing you, you would have known about it by now. For a start, we wouldn't be having this conversation, because it would be a waste of my time and my time is very precious. Do you understand what I'm saying?'

Yes, she understood. She thought how *forbidding* he seemed. From the way he was behaving, nobody would ever have guessed they'd once been lovers. She had seen his ruthless streak before—it had been essential in his role as bodyguard to one of Russia's richest men. But around her he had always been playful—the way she'd sometimes imagined a lion might be if it ever allowed you to get close enough to pet it. Until their affair had finished, and then he had acted as if she was dead to him.

Was that why he was doing this—to pay her back for having turned down his proposal of marriage, even though at the time she had known it was the only thing she *could* do?

She must not let him intimidate her, nor allow him to see how terrified she was of losing her livelihood. Because Loukas was the ultimate predator…he saw a weakness and then moved in for the kill. That was what he had been trained to do. She clasped her hands together and looked at him. 'So why are we having this conversation?'

'Because I have a reputation for turning around failing companies, which is what I intend to do with this one.'

'How?'

He was looking at her calculatingly, like a butcher weighing a piece of meat on a set of scales. 'You are no longer a teenager, Jess,' he said softly. 'And neither are the girls who first bought the watch. You are no longer a tennis star, either—you are what's known in the business as a has-been. And there's no point glowering at me like that. I am simply stating a fact. You were taken on because of who you were—a shining talent whose dreams were shattered. You were the tragic heroine. The sporty blonde who kept on smiling through the pain. Young girls wanted to be you.'

'But not any more?' she said slowly.

'I'm afraid not. You're trading on something which has gone. The world has moved on, but you've stayed exactly the same. Same old shots of you with the ponytail and the pearls and the Capri pants and the neat blouses.' His eyes glittered. 'I get bored just thinking about them.'

She nodded, her heart beating very hard, because it hurt to have him talk to her this way. To have her life condensed into a sad little story which left him feeling 'bored'. She met his black eyes and tried to keep the pain from her face. 'So what are you planning to do about it?'

'I am giving you the opportunity to breathe some life back into your career—and to boost Lulu's flagging sales.'

She wished she'd taken her raincoat off, because her body was beginning to grow hot beneath that scorching stare. She tried to keep her voice calm. To forget that this was Loukas. To try to imagine that it was the previous CEO sitting there, a man with a cut-glass accent who used to ask her for tennis tips for his young daughter. 'How?'

He leaned back in his chair, his outward air of relaxation mocking the churned-up way she was feeling inside.

'By giving you a new look—one which reflects the woman you are now and not the girl you used to be. We make you over. New hairstyle. New clothes. We do the whole Cinderella thing and then reveal you to the public. The nation's sweetheart all grown up. Just imagine the resulting publicity that would generate.' His eyes glittered. 'Priceless.'

She shifted uncomfortably in her chair. 'You make me sound like a commodity, Loukas,' she said, in a low voice.

He laughed. 'But that's exactly what you are. Why would you think any differently? You sell images of yourself to promote a product—of course you're a commodity. You just happen to be one which has reached its sell-by date,

I'm afraid—unless you're prepared to mix it up a bit.'

She met the hard gleam of his eyes and a real sense of sadness washed over her. Because despite the way their affair had ended, there had still been a portion of her heart which made her think of him with…

With what?

Affection?

No. Affection was too mild a description for the feelings she'd had for Loukas Sarantos. She had *loved* him despite knowing that they were completely wrong for each other. She had loved him more than he'd ever known because she'd been trained to keep her feelings locked away, and she had taken all her training seriously. The way they'd parted had filled her with regret and she'd be lying if she tried to deny that sometimes she thought about him with a deep ache in her heart and a very different kind of ache in her body. Who didn't lie in bed at night sometimes, wondering how different life might have been if you'd taken a different path?

But now? Now he was making her feel angry, frustrated and stretched to breaking point. He made her want to pummel her fists against him, but most of all he made her want to kiss him. That was the most shameful thing of all—that she was still in some kind of physical thrall to him. She wanted him to cover her mouth with one of his hot kisses. To make her melt. To feel that first sharp and piercing wave of pleasure as he entered her and have it blot out the rest of the world.

She stared into his mocking eyes, telling herself that her desire was irrelevant. More than that, it was dangerous, because it unsettled her and made her want things she knew were wrong. No good was ever going to come of their continued association. He wanted to change her. To make her into someone she wasn't. And all the while making her aware of her own failures, while he showcased his own spectacular success.

Was that what *she* wanted?

'Why are you doing this, Loukas?'

'Because I can.' He smiled. 'Why else?'

And suddenly she saw the Loukas of old. The man who could become as still as a piece of dark and forbidding rock. Foreboding whispered over her skin as she rose to her feet. 'This isn't going to work,' she said. 'I just can't imagine having any kind of working association with you. I'm sorry.'

'You should be.' His voice was silky. 'I've had my lawyers take a good look at your contract. Refuse this job and you aren't in line for any compensation. You leave here empty-handed. Have you thought about that?'

Briefly, Jessica imagined Hannah, happily backpacking in Thailand. Hannah who had defied all expectations to land herself a place at Cambridge University. Her teenage half-sister on the other side of the world, blissfully oblivious to what was going on back home. What would she say if she knew that her future security was about to be cut from under her, by a black-eyed man with a heart of stone?

But as she bent to pick up her handbag she told herself that she would think of something. There were opportunities for employment in her native Cornwall—admittedly not many, but she would look at whatever was going. She could turn her hand to plenty of other things. She could cook and clean or even work in a shop. Her embroidery was selling locally and craftwork was becoming more popular, so couldn't she do more of that? Better that than to stay for a second longer in a room where the air seemed to be suffocating her. Where the man she had once loved seemed to be taking real pleasure from watching her squirm.

Her fingers curled around the strap of her handbag. 'You might want to think about changing your own image rather than concentrating on mine,' she said quietly. 'That macho attitude of yours is so passé.'

'You think so?' he drawled, leaning back in his chair and surveying her from between narrowed eyes. 'I've always found it particularly effective. Especially with women. Most of them seem to get turned on by the caveman approach. You certainly did.'

With his middle finger, he began to draw a tiny circle on the contract and Jessica found herself remembering when he used to touch her skin that way. The way he used to drift his fingertip over her body with such light and exquisite precision. She'd been unable to resist him and she wondered whether any woman would be capable of resistance if Loukas Sarantos had them in his sights.

And suddenly he looked up and smiled—a cruel, cold smile—as if he knew exactly what was running through her mind.

'Yes,' he said softly. 'I still want you, Jessica. I didn't realise quite how much until I saw you today. And you'd better understand that these days I get everything I want. So I'll give you time to reconsider your decision, but I'm warning you that my patience is not infinite. And I won't wait long.'

'Don't hold your breath,' she said, meeting his eyes with a defiant look which lasted only as long as it took her to walk out of his office, her heart pounding as she headed for the elevator.

He didn't follow her. Had she really thought he would? Had there been a trace of the old Jessica who thought he might rise to his feet and cover the distance between them with a few purposeful strides, just like in the old days? *Yes, there had.* And wasn't part of her still craving that kind of masterful behaviour? Of course it was. What woman could remain immune to all that brooding power, coupled with the steely new patina which his wealth had given him?

She shook her head as she left the building, realising that Suzy had been right. He *was* dangerous and the way he made her feel was more dangerous still. Far better that she walked away now and left him in the past, where he belonged.

Hurrying through the emerging rush hour, she caught the train to Cornwall with seconds to spare, but the usually breathtaking journey was shrouded in darkness. The January evening was cold and rain lashed against the carriage windows, seeming to echo her gloomy mood.

She leant her head back against the seat, wondering if she was crazy to have turned her back on a job which had been her security for so long. Yet surely she'd be crazier still to put herself in a situation where Loukas held all the power.

Her love for him might have been replaced by a mixture of anger and frustration—but she was far from immune to him. She couldn't deny the sharp kick of desire when she looked at him, or her squirming sense of frustration. And if that frustration had been unexpectedly powerful, was that really so surprising? Because there had been nobody else since Loukas. No other lover in eight long years. He had been her first man and the only man. Wasn't that ridiculous? And unfashionable? He'd accused her of being stuck in a rut, but he didn't know the half of it.

Because nobody had come close to making her feel the way Loukas had done. She'd *tried* to have relationships with other men but they had left her feeling cold. She stared out of the window as the train pulled into the darkness of a rain-lashed Bodmin station. Other men had made her feel nothing, while her Greek lover had made her feel everything.

Just under an hour later and she was home. But the sight of the little Atlantic-facing house which usually filled her with feelings of sanctuary tonight did no such thing. Rods of rain hit her like icy arrows as she got out of the taxi. The crash of the ocean was deafening but for once she took no pleasure from it. Tonight the sound seemed lonely and haunting and full of foreboding.

And of course, the house was empty. She seemed to rattle around in it without the noisy presence of her half-sister. Jessica listened to the unusual sound of silence as the front door slammed closed behind her. She missed Hannah. Missed her a lot. Yet who would have thought it? It certainly hadn't been sunshine and laughter when Jessica's father had split from her mother, to marry his long-term mistress who was already pregnant with his daughter, Hannah.

Jessica had been badly hurt by her parents' bitter divorce and the news that she was going to have a stepmother and a brand-new baby sister had filled her with jealousy and dread. There had been plenty of tensions in their 'blended' family, but somehow they had survived—even when Jessica's mum had died soon after and the villagers had whispered that she'd never got over her broken heart. Jessica had tried to form a good relationship with her stepmother and to improve the one she had with her perfectionist father. Until that terrible day when an avalanche had left both girls orphaned and alone.

After that, it had been a case of sink, or swim. They'd *had* to get along, because there had been no alternative. Jessica had been eighteen and Hannah just ten when the policeman had knocked on the door with that terrible expression on his face. The authorities had wanted to take Hannah into care but Jessica had fought hard to adopt her. But worse was to come when Jessica realised that her father had been living a lie—spending money on the back of her future earnings, which were never going to materialise. The lawyers had sat her down and told her that their affluent lifestyle had been nothing but an illusion, funded by money they didn't have.

She'd been at her wits' end, wondering how she could support herself and Hannah, because there was precious little left after the big house had been sold. That was why the Lulu job had been such a lifesaver. It had given her money to pay the bills, yes, but, more preciously, it had given her the time to try to mother her heartbroken half-sister in a way that a regular job could never have done.

She had learnt to cook and had planted vegetables. And even though the plants hadn't done very well in the salty and wind-lashed Cornish garden, just the act of nurturing something had brought the two sisters closer together. She had attended every single school open evening and had always been there for Hannah, no matter what. She'd tried not to freak out when the young teenager was discovered smoking dope at a party, telling her that everyone was allowed one mistake. She'd stayed calm the year Hannah had flunked all her exams because of some school bad-boy who'd been giving her the runaround. Instead, she had quietly emphasised the importance of learning and told her how much she regretted her own patchy education—all sacrificed in the name of tennis. And somehow love had grown out of a relationship which had begun so badly.

Jessica had cried when she'd seen Hannah off at Heathrow Airport just before Christmas, with that ridiculously bulky rucksack dwarfing her slender frame, but she had waited until the plane had taken off before she had allowed the tears to fall. Not just because she kept her emotions hidden as a matter of habit, but because she knew this was how it was supposed to be. She knew that saying goodbye was part of life.

And today she'd said goodbye to a part-time modelling career which had never been intended to last. She'd had a good run for her money but now it was time to try something new.

Jessica bit her lip as the rain beat down against the window and tried to block out the memories of Loukas's mocking face. She would think of something.

She had to.

CHAPTER THREE

BUT FATE HAD a habit of screwing things up when you least expected it and three things happened in rapid succession which made Jessica regret her decision to walk away from Loukas Sarantos and his job offer. Her washing machine packed up, her car died, and then Hannah had her wallet stolen while swimming off a beach in Thailand.

Jessica's first thought had been sheer panic when she'd heard the teenager's choking tears on the other end of the line, until she started thinking how much worse it could have been. And once her fears had calmed down to a manageable level, she felt nothing but frustration. But it was a wake-up call and the series of unexpected expenses forced her to take a cold, hard look at her finances and to face up to them with a sinking feeling of inevitability. Was she really deluded enough to think she could manage to live by selling a few framed pieces of *embroidery*? Why, that would barely cover the electricity bill.

She stood at the window, watching the white plume of the waves crashing down over the rocky beach. There *were* alternatives, she knew that. She could sell this house and move somewhere without a lusted-after sea view, which added so much money to the property's value. But this was her security. Her rock. When they'd had to sell their childhood home, this had become a place of safety to retreat to when chaos threatened and she hadn't planned on leaving it any time soon. Especially now. She'd read somewhere that young people were left feeling rootless and insecure if the family home was sold when they went off to college. How could she possibly do that to Hannah, who had already lost so much in her short life?

She thought about what Loukas had said to her, his words both a threat and a promise. *I won't wait long.*

She picked up the phone and dialled the number before she had a chance to change her mind and asked to speak him. He's probably no longer interested, she thought, her heart pounding loudly. I've probably offended his macho pride by making him wait.

'Jess.' His deep voice fired into her thoughts and sent them scattering.

'Loukas?' she questioned stupidly, because who else could make her shiver with erotic recall, just by saying her name?

'I'd like to say that this is a surprise,' he said softly. 'But it isn't. I've been waiting for your call, although it hasn't come as quickly as I would have expected.' There was a pause. 'What do you want?'

Jessica closed her eyes. He knew exactly what she wanted—was he going to make her crawl in order to get it? She opened them again and saw another wave crash down onto the rocks. Maybe she *was* going to have to swallow her pride—but that didn't mean she needed to fall to the ground and lick his boots.

'I've been thinking about what you said and on reflection...' She drew in a deep breath. 'On reflection, it does seem too good an opportunity to turn down. So I've decided to accept the offer—if it's still on the table.'

At the other end of the line Loukas clenched and unclenched his free hand, because her cool response frustrated him far more than her opposition had done. He liked her when she was fighting and fiery, because fire he could easily extinguish. Making ice melt was different—that took much longer—and he had neither the time nor the inclination to make his seduction of Jessica Cartwright into a long-term project. She was just another tick on the list he was working his way down. His heart clenched with bitterness even while his body clenched with lust. She was something unfinished he needed to file away in the box marked 'over'. He wanted her body. To sate himself until he'd had his fill. And then he wanted to walk away and forget her.

'Loukas,' she was saying, her voice reminding him of all the erotic little things she used to whisper. She had been an incredibly quick learner, he remembered, his groin hardening uncomfortably. His innocent virgin had quickly become the most sensual lover he'd ever known.

'Loukas, are you still there?'

'Yes, I'm still here,' he said unevenly. 'And we need to talk.'

'We're talking now.'

'Not like this. Face to face.'

'But I thought…'

Her voice tailed off and Loukas realised that he *liked* the heady kick of power which her uncertainty gave him. Suddenly he wanted her submissive. He wanted to be the one calling all the shots, as once she had called them. 'What did you think, Jess?' he questioned softly. 'That you wouldn't need to see me again?'

He could hear her clearing her throat.

'Well, yes,' she said. 'I always deal with the advertising agency and the stylist—and the photographer, of course. That's what usually happens.'

'Well, you're wrong. None of this is *usual*, because I am in charge now. I like a hands-on approach—and if the previous CEO had possessed any sense, he would have done the same. You need to meet with our new advertising agency and for that you need to be in London. I'll have someone at Lulu book you into a hotel.'

'Okay.' She cleared her throat again. 'When did you have in mind?'

'As soon as possible. A car will be sent to pick you up this afternoon.'

'That soon?' Her voice sounded breathless. 'You're expecting me to be ready in a couple of hours?'

'Are you saying you can't? That you have other commitments?'

'I might have,' she stalled and something made her say it, though she wasn't quite sure what. 'I might have a date.'

There was a pause. 'Then cancel it, *koukla mou.*'

As his words filtered down the line, Jessica froze, because even though it had been a long time since she'd heard it, the Greek term sounded thrillingly familiar. My doll. That was what it meant. Jessica bit her lip. He used to say it to her a lot, but never with quite such contempt. Once she had trembled with pleasure when he had whispered it into her ear but now the words seemed to mean different things. They seemed tinged with foreboding rather than affection.

'And if I don't?' she questioned defiantly.

'Why not take a little advice, mmm? Let's not get this relationship off on a bad footing,' he said. 'Your initial refusal to cooperate irritated me but your game-playing is starting to irritate me even more. Don't make the mistake of overestimating your own appeal, Jess—and don't push me too far.'

'And is that...' she drew in a deep breath '...supposed to intimidate me?'

'It's supposed to make you aware of where we both stand.'

There was a pause and his voice suddenly changed gear. It became sultry and velvety. It sounded *irresistible*.

'Do you really have a date tonight, Jess?'

She wanted to say yes—to tell him that some gorgeous man was coming round to take her out. A man who was carrying a big bunch of flowers and wearing a soppy grin on his face. And that after champagne and oysters, he would bring her back here and make mad, passionate love to her.

But the vision disintegrated before her eyes, because the thought of any man other than Loukas touching her left her cold. And how sad was that?

'No,' she said flatly. 'I don't.'

'Thavmassios.' His voice dipped with satisfaction. 'Then I will see you later. Oh, and make sure you bring your passport.'

'What for?'

'What do you think? The new team want to use an exotic location for the shoot,' he said impatiently. 'Just *do* it, will you, Jess? I don't intend to run everything past you for your approval—that's not how it works. It's certainly not how *I* work.'

He terminated the connection and Jessica found herself listening frustratedly to a hollow silence. But there was nothing she could do about it. She was going to have to change her image, if that was what it took. She would accept the makeover and smile for the camera and do her best to hold onto her contract for as long as she could. But that was all she would do. She knew what else he wanted and that certainly wasn't written into the deal.

She didn't have to sleep with him.

She closed all the windows, turned off the heating and emptied the fridge and two hours later a sleek black limousine arrived to collect her, slowly negotiating its way along the narrow, unmade road which led to her house.

It felt disorientating to hand her bags to the uniformed driver and slide onto the back seat as the powerful vehicle pulled away. During the journey she tried to read but it was impossible to concentrate. Her mind kept taking her back to places she didn't want to go—and the past was her biggest no-go destination. She stared out of the window and watched as the

Cornish countryside gave way to Devon and found herself thinking about Loukas and the way he used to come and watch her practising, way before they'd got to know each other.

The public footpath used to cross right by their tennis court when she had lived at the big house, and she would look up with a fast-beating heart to find a dark and brooding figure standing there. It used to drive her father potty, but it was a public space and he could hardly order the Greek bodyguard away. Not that he would have dared try. Loukas Sarantos wasn't the kind of man you would order to do anything. She'd been a bit scared of him herself. He had been so dark and effortlessly powerful, and the way she'd caught him looking at her legs had made her feel… It was difficult to put into words the way he'd made her feel. She had tried very hard to steer her thoughts away from him and to concentrate on the fact that she double-faulted every time he watched her.

'He will destroy your career!' her father had roared and Jessica had promised that she wouldn't see him—though at that point he hadn't even asked her out.

And then she'd run into him in the village when her father had taken his wife and Hannah up to London and Jessica had been given a rare day to herself. She hadn't gone near a tennis ball all day and that had felt like a liberation in itself. She'd been feeling restless and rebellious and had wandered to the nearby shop to buy herself chocolate. Her hand had been hovering over the purple-wrapped bar when a deeply accented voice had said,

'Do you really think you should?'

She had looked up into a pair of mocking black eyes and something had happened. It had felt like being touched by magic. As if her heart had caught fire. She didn't remember what they'd said, only that he'd flirted with her and she'd flirted back in a way which had seemed to come as easily as breathing—because how could you not flirt with a man like Loukas? He had been exotic, different, edgy and enigmatic, but that hadn't mattered. Nothing had mattered other than the urgent need to be near him.

She'd offered to show him the famous borehole which was set in the surrounding cliffs like the imprint of a giant cannonball. His stride had been longer than hers and she remembered the wind whipping her ponytail as they'd stared down into the dark hollow.

He'd told her that it reminded him of the diamond mine owned by his Russian boss, but she hadn't been particularly interested in hearing about diamonds. All she'd wanted was for him to kiss her, and he must have known that, because mid-sentence he'd stopped and and said, 'Oh, so *that's* what you want, is it, little Miss Tennis?' And he had caught her in his arms and his dark head had moved slowly towards hers and she had been lost.

The kiss had sealed a deal she hadn't realised they were making. Jessica had wanted to have sex with him instantly, but something had made her pull back. Because even though she'd wanted him very badly, instinct had told her that he was a man used to women falling at his feet and she should take it slowly. And somehow she had.

Two weeks had felt like an eternity before she'd let him take her virginity, and if part of her had wondered if all that sensual promise could possibly be met, she'd discovered that it could. Oh, it had. For someone who'd spent her life relying on her body to help her win, who had worked through all the pain and injuries, she had now discovered a completely different use for it. An intense pleasure which had made the rest of the world fade away. He had made her gasp. He had made her heart want to burst with joy. She had been hooked on sex and hooked on him.

They had snatched what moments they could and maybe the subterfuge had only added to the excitement. He'd told her his boss wouldn't approve of their relationship and Jessica had known her father would have hit the roof if he'd known. But that hadn't stopped her falling in love with Loukas, even though she would sooner have flown to the moon than showed it. Until the night when she'd blurted it out to him. She could remember even now the slow way he had smiled at her...

And then her father had found her contraceptive pills. Even now she cringed at the humiliating scene which had followed. She should have told him it was none of his business, but she had been barely eighteen and had spent her life being told what to do by someone for whom ambition had been everything. He had confronted Loukas. Told him he had *taken advantage* of his daughter, and had threatened to go to his boss. And what had Loukas done? She bit her lip, because even now it hurt to remember him squaring up his shoulders, as if he'd been just about to step into the fray. In a gruff and unfamiliar voice he had offered to marry her.

And her response? She had said no, because what else could she have said? She'd known he had only been asking her because he'd felt it was the right thing to do and she couldn't bear to trap this proud man in a relationship he'd never intended. Had she been able to see the two of them together—even ten years down the line? No, she hadn't. And if she was being honest, her career had been too important for her to want to risk it on the random throw of an emotional dice. She'd been working towards being a champion since she'd been four years old. Had she really been prepared to throw all that away because Loukas had been offering something out of a misplaced sense of duty?

But her heart had been breaking as she'd ended their affair, even though she'd known it was the right thing to do. She remembered the way he had looked at her, an expression of slowly dawning comprehension hardening his black eyes, before he had laughed. A low, bitter laugh—as if she had just confirmed something he'd already known.

She remembered the way she'd felt as he had

turned his back on her and walked away—a clear bright pain which had seemed to consume her. That was the last time she'd seen him, until the moment she'd walked into the penthouse office at Lulu's—a bodyguard no longer but an international tycoon. Jessica shook her head in slight disbelief. How on earth had he managed that?

The slowing pace of the traffic made her realise that they'd hit central London and that the limousine was drawing up outside the Vinoly Hotel, a place she'd never stayed in before. The company usually put her up in the infinitely larger Granchester whenever she was in London and she wondered why they'd sent her here.

The driver opened the door. 'Mr Sarantos says to inform you that a suite has been booked in your name and that you are to order anything you need.'

Jessica nodded and walked into the interior of the plush hotel, whose foyer was dominated by a red velvet sofa in the shape of a giant pair of lips. A Perspex chair on a gilt chain was suspended from the ceiling and impossibly cool-looking young people in jeans and expensive jackets were sprawled around, drinking coffee and tapping away furiously on their laptops.

The receptionist smiled as she handed her a key card and an envelope. 'This was delivered for you earlier,' she said. 'We hope you have a pleasant stay with us, Miss Cartwright. The valet will show you to your suite.'

Jessica didn't have to look at the envelope to know who it was from. Her heart was racing as she recognised Loukas's handwriting— bold and flowing and unlike any other she'd ever seen. She knew his education had been patchy. He'd taught himself to read and write, but had ended up at the age of seventeen without a single qualification, other than a driving licence. But that was pretty much all she knew because he had been notoriously tight-lipped about his childhood. A sombre look used to darken his face whenever she dared ask, so that in the end she gave up trying—because wasn't it easier to grab at rainbows rather than chase after storms?

She waited until she was in her suite before opening the envelope, so intent on reading it that she barely noticed the stark decor of the room. Loukas's message was fairly stark, too.

I trust you had a good journey. Meet me in the dining room downstairs at eight. In the wardrobe you will find a black dress. Wear it.

Jessica's mouth dried. It was an explicit request which sounded almost sexual. Had that been his intention? Did he plan to make her skin prickle with excitement the moment she read it, or to make her feel the molten pull of desire? Walking over to the line of wardrobe doors, she pulled open the first to find a dress hanging there—noting without any sense of surprise that it was made by a renowned designer. It was deceptively simple—a masterpiece fashioned from heavy silk and Jessica could instantly see how exquisitely it was cut. She thought how beautifully it would hang, and wasn't there a tiny part of her which longed to wear it? Because it was a sexy dress. A woman's dress. The kind of garment which would be worn in the knowledge that later a man would remove it.

Heart pounding, she turned away from the temptation it presented and everything else it symbolised and stared defiantly at her own belongings. She resented his peremptory tone and much else besides. He had no right to order her what to wear. The job hadn't even started and already he was acting as if he owned her. Being summoned here within the space of a few hours was one thing, but no way was Loukas going to decide on her wardrobe.

By eight she had showered and changed and was heading down towards the restaurant. Outwardly composed, she announced her arrival to the maître d' but her fingers were trembling as she was shown across the candlelit room to where Loukas was already seated.

This time she was prepared for his impact, but it made little difference to her reaction. Illuminated by the soft glow of candlelight, he was occupying the best table in the room and looking completely at home—as if he owned the space and all that surrounded him. She saw the unmistakable darkening of his eyes as she approached, but the flicker of a nerve at his temple indicated a flash of anger, rather than lust.

And suddenly she began to regret the determination with which she had pulled on a cream-coloured dress which fell demurely to just below the knee. She knew she must appear faintly colourless among the exotically clothed women in the room, but surely maintaining her independence was more important than blending in with the slick, city crowd. More importantly, it would send out a subliminal message to her former lover, telling him that she was still very much her own woman, no matter how much she needed the job.

He said nothing until she had been seated and presented with a menu, but he waved the waiter away with an impatient hand, and when he spoke his voice felt like the brushing of dark velvet all the way down her spine.

'I thought I told you to wear the black dress?'

She met his gaze with the imperturbable stare which had once served her so well on the tennis court. 'No woman likes to be told what dress to put on, Loukas.'

'I beg to differ.' His voice was soft. Dangerously soft. 'Why would you object to wearing a costly gown which would make you look amazing?'

'Because I don't want or need your costly gowns.'

'I see.' Reflectively, his finger moved across his lips. 'And presumably you chose that bland-looking outfit to ensure I wouldn't be attracted to you?'

Jessica felt her cheeks grow hot. She might not have dressed to impress but she knew she looked neat and smart, and it hurt to hear him say something unnecessarily cruel like that. Was that the reason she started defending herself—why she was foolish enough to try? 'You didn't used to complain about the colour of my clothes.'

'That's because I was young and I didn't care what you wore. Actually, I was more concerned about getting you naked.' He paused to slant her a flinty smile. 'Something which was never a problem after your initial reluctance.'

'Well, at least that side of things need no longer concern you.'

'"That side of things"?' he mimicked in amusement. 'Don't be coy, Jess. If you're talking about sex, why not just come out and say it?'

'Okay, I will.' Jessica waved her menu in front of him, pleased that the candlelight camouflaged her sudden blush. 'And sex isn't on the menu, I'm afraid.'

He leaned back in his chair and smiled. 'Your defiance excites me,' he said. 'Mainly because I wasn't expecting it.'

'No?'

'No.' He shook his head. 'I thought you might be happy to put on a dress which your average female would lust after.'

'Maybe I'm not your average female.'

'No, maybe you're not.' His lashes came down to half shield the ebony gleam of his eyes. 'I was also wondering whether or not you would be *compliant* and it gives me a perverse kind of pleasure that you weren't.'

'Really?' She raised her eyebrows. 'And why's that?'

He smiled. 'Because if you present a man with a woman who is disobedient, then he is conditioned to want to *tame* her. To sublimate her unruly temperament. And that is something which fills me with anticipation and excitement.'

His words washed over her—edged with an eroticism she couldn't ignore. And suddenly Jessica felt out of her depth. As if she'd underestimated him. As if she'd unwittingly signed up for something more than a change of image and a brand-new advertising campaign. He looked so powerful as he sat there. As if he was playing a game, only she didn't know what that game was. Because although this man looked like Loukas—a very polished

Loukas—she realised that he was a stranger to her.

He had always been a stranger to her, she realised with a sinking heart. Hadn't he always kept a side of himself locked away?

But her face betrayed nothing, her smile as polite as if they were discussing nothing more controversial than the January weather. 'Do you really think it's acceptable to invite a woman for dinner and then to talk about taming her?'

This time his smile was edged with definite danger. 'Doesn't that turn you on—a masterful man taking control of a stubborn woman? I must say, it has always been one of my enduring fantasies, my little Ice Queen.'

Ice Queen. Jessica didn't react to that either. It was a long time since she'd heard the term which had dogged her junior years as a player and followed her onto the senior circuit. She had hated it, although her father had approved. He'd said it meant she'd achieved what she'd set out to achieve—a cold unflappability. Or rather, what *he* had set out to achieve. All Jessica knew was that being cold didn't make you popular with the other players, even if the ability to keep your feelings hidden made you a formidable opponent. Not showing when you were angry, or sad, or rattled had distinct advantages when you were playing tennis—just not in real life. It made people think you had no real feelings. It made them call you Ice Queen. And it made men like Loukas Sarantos interested in you because they thought you presented the ultimate challenge.

'I'm not interested in your sexual fantasies,' she said quietly.

'Honestly?'

'No. What I'm interested in,' she said, dragging her thoughts away with an effort, 'is how you've become so incredibly rich.'

'Not right now,' he said, with silky resignation—as if he'd been expecting the question a whole lot sooner. 'Here comes the waiter. Let's deal with him first. Do you know what you want to eat? Perhaps you would like me to order for you?'

Jessica bristled. He was doing it again, just as he'd tried to do with the dress. That whole command *thing* which was teetering on the brink of domination. She was perfectly capable of ordering her own food and she ought to tell him that, but, faced with the prospect of deciphering a long menu beneath a gaze which was making her feel so *conflicted*, Jessica shrugged her acceptance.

She listened while he quizzed the sommelier and the waiter with a knowledge he clearly hadn't acquired overnight. It was strange seeing him like this in public—giving orders where in the past he had taken them. As strange as seeing him in his expensive suit. She was left feeling dazed when they were alone once more and two glasses of white wine had been poured for them. All she knew was that she mustn't let him dominate her. That she needed to start asserting herself, just as she had done so often on the tennis court.

'So are you going to tell me?' she persisted, with a determination which seemed to well up from somewhere deep inside her. From the far end of the room a jazz pianist began playing something haunting and sultry and the music seemed to invade her senses as Jessica stared at him. 'What has happened to you to make you the man you are today, Loukas?'

CHAPTER FOUR

LOUKAS STARED INTO Jessica's aquamarine eyes—as cool as any swimming pool he'd ever dived into—and wondered how to answer her question. His instinct was to tell her that his past and his career trajectory were none of her business. Was her sudden interest sparked because she was turned on by his obvious wealth like most of her sex?

Yet in a way she had been partly responsible for the dramatic turnaround in his fortunes, though not in a way which either of them could have predicted. Her rejection of him had cut deep. Deeper than he could ever have anticipated. Her cool dismissal of his proposal had kicked like a horse at his pride and his heart, leaving him angry and empty. And bewildered. Because hadn't he once vowed to himself that never again would he give a woman the opportunity to hurt him?

'I stopped working for Dimitri Makarov,' he said.

She frowned. 'You mean, you got tired of being a bodyguard?'

Loukas gave a hard smile in response to her question. Yes, he had grown tired of living life through someone else. Of standing on the sidelines. Of always having to abide by someone else's rules and someone else's timetable. And waiting—always waiting.

'It was time for a change,' he said, watching the way her hair gleamed in the candlelight. 'I didn't want to carry on indefinitely and at that stage Dimitri's personal life was so out of control that the two of us were living like vampires. He never went to bed before dawn and, as a consequence, neither did I. We spent our life in casinos and then we'd take a plane to another country and another casino, grabbing sleep where we could.'

His Russian boss had been out of control—and so had he. Each of them running from their particular demons and seeking refuge in the bottom of a whisky glass. On the rebound from Jessica, Loukas had gone from woman to woman, despising them all no matter how much they professed to love him, because hadn't he proved once and for all that you could never believe a woman when she said she loved you?

And then one morning he had woken up and looked in the mirror, barely able to recognise the ravaged face staring back, and had known that something needed to change. Or rather, that *he* needed to change. 'It was time for something new,' he finished flatly. 'A new direction.'

He watched while she took a sip of her wine—a wine as cool and as pale as she was.

'So what did you do?' she questioned. 'Go to college?'

Loukas couldn't hold back the bitterness of his answering laugh, but he waited while their food was placed before them—fish and vegetables stacked into intricate towers standing in puddles of shiny orange sauce. Why the hell could you never get simple food these days? he wondered fleetingly. 'No, Jess— I didn't go to *college*,' he said sarcastically. 'Those kinds of opportunities aren't really a good fit with someone like me. I started working as a bouncer at a big nightclub in New York.'

She narrowed her eyes. He thought she

looked disappointed. Was that still too *thuggish* an occupation for someone of her delicate sensibilities to accept?

'And what was that like?' she asked politely, like someone making small talk at a cocktail party.

'It was like every man's fantasy,' he said softly and now he could see the surprise in her eyes, and yes, the hurt—and suddenly he found that he was enjoying himself and that he wanted to hurt her some more. To hurt her as she had hurt him. 'It's a power trip to be in a position like that,' he drawled softly. 'It gives you a kick to turn away people with overstuffed wallets who ask if you know who they are. Not a particularly admirable admission—but true. And women love bouncers. *Really* love them,' he finished deliberately. 'It's one of the perks of the job.'

She had been sawing at a piece of pumpkin on her plate, but suddenly she put her fork down and he noticed that her hand was trembling. And that was unusual, he thought with satisfaction, because Jess had always had the steadiest hands of anyone he'd ever known. Hands that could throw a tennis ball up to a certain height with pinpoint accuracy. Hands that could smash a ball into kingdom come. He could see the faint uncertainty in her eyes as she asked the inevitable question.

'And I suppose there must have been, well… *lots* of women?'

He shrugged, because if a female asked you a question as dumb as that, then they deserved to hear the answer. He thought about the pieces of paper slipped into his hand or stuffed into the pockets of his jacket. About waking up in vast bedrooms on the Upper East Side with some sinewy heiress riding him until he cried out. The tiny thong he'd found stuffed in his jacket pocket when he'd been going through airport security and the knowing wink of the uniformed official when he'd seen it. He smiled. 'Enough,' he said succinctly.

'But bouncers don't get to be big bosses,' she said, her words sounding forced and rushed, as if she suddenly wanted to change the subject. 'They don't get to own companies the size of Lulu.'

'No, they don't.' He picked up his wine and swirled it round in the glass, thinking that at one time he could have lived for a month on the money this bottle had cost.

'So, how…' she waved her hand through the

air, as if he owned the expensive restaurant too '...did you get all this?'

He drank some wine. 'I started to hear rumours that Dimitri's new protection was not to be trusted. And then one day his secretary contacted me and begged me to help. I'd left months before and didn't want to get involved, but she was worried sick—crying down the phone and telling me she thought he was in danger. So I travelled to Paris to talk to him but by that time he had become so big that he thought he was invincible. He agreed to see me, but he wouldn't believe any of the things I'd discovered about the people he was associating with.' His mouth hardened into a grim line. 'Dimitri only ever listened when it was something he wanted to hear. So I gave up trying and planned to take a flight out of the city that same night.'

'But something...stopped you?' she said, breaking into the sudden silence as his words tailed away. And suddenly her eyes were very wide, as if she'd seen something in his face which she wasn't supposed to see.

'Yes, something stopped me,' he agreed grimly. 'It transpired that his new bodyguard was connected to a gang who were on the brink of stealing from my ex Russian boss, and my presence in the city was seen as a bonus, because I knew more about Dimitri's affairs than anyone else. And that pretty much sealed my fate. They captured me on the way to Charles de Gaulle airport.'

'They *captured* you?' she said, only now her voice had a break in it, as if she didn't quite believe the words she was saying. 'What… what happened?'

For a moment the only sound was the tinkly little flourish which came at the end of the jazz player's song and the smattering of applause which followed.

He shrugged. 'They beat me and threatened me. Said I would die unless I told them what they wanted to know.'

'They said you would *die*?' Her face had gone completely pale.

'It's the underworld's way of suggesting you hand over the information they want,' he said sardonically.

And…did you?'

'Are you crazy?' He picked up his glass but this time he didn't drink from it. 'I was expecting to die anyway, so I was damned if I was going to tell them anything first.'

She was blinking at him as if she'd never really seen him before. 'You thought you were going to *die*?'

He heard the frightened squeak of her voice and thought how protected she'd always been. But then, most people had been protected from the kind of worlds he had inhabited. 'Yeah,' he agreed with soft sarcasm. 'Just like something out of a film isn't it, Jess?'

She shook her head, as if his flippancy was inappropriate. 'So what saved you?'

He shrugged. Tonight the wine tasted good, just as everything had tasted good when he'd first been released. He remembered falling to his knees on the dank concrete of that underground car park with drops of blood dripping darkly from his nose, telling himself that never again would he take anything for granted. But he had, of course. He'd discovered that gratitude didn't last very long.

'Dimitri started to believe that maybe I had been speaking the truth and some hunch made him have me followed to the airport. They got to me in the nick of time, and when I was brought back to his place and he saw the state I was in, I think it made him realise he couldn't carry on the way he was—something his secretary had been telling him for a long time. And he gave me diamonds as a reward for what I'd done.'

'Diamonds?' she questioned blankly.

'He owns one of Russia's biggest mines. He gave me jewels which were priceless and he told me to learn to love them.' He saw her flinch at the word, as if he had just sworn. And maybe he had. Maybe it was easier to think of love as a profanity than as something which was real. He remembered Dimitri's words as he had run his fingers through the glittering cascade. *Learn to love these cold stones, my friend, for they are easier to love than women.*

'And did you?' Jess's cool voice broke into his thoughts. 'Learn to love them?'

He smiled. 'I did. It's easy to love something which is so valuable, but I developed a genuine interest in them. They began to fascinate me. I liked their beauty and perfection and the way all that value could be hidden in the pocket of a man's jacket. I liked the fact that they only ever increase in value and I cannot deny that it gave me pleasure to realise their power over people. Women will do pretty much anything for diamonds,' he said deliberately.

'Will they?' came her light answer, as if she didn't care.

'Some I sold and others I kept,' he continued. 'I'm planning to use some of them as the centrepiece of the new launch. No more wristwatches for you from now on, my blue-eyed doll. You will wear my diamonds, Jess.'

She moved the palm of her hand so that it lay on her breastbone, like someone who had grown suddenly short of breath, but the movement only drew attention to the little pulse which was hammering at the base of her throat.

'So was…' she seemed to pick her words carefully '…was the fact that you bought Lulu just a coincidence?'

'In what way?'

She opened her lips slowly, like someone afraid of setting off a verbal landmine.

'You didn't just buy Lulu because I was working there?'

He gave a soft laugh. 'What do you think?'

'I'm not…I'm not sure.'

But Loukas knew she was lying. Would the Lulu takeover have been *quite* so enticing if she hadn't been involved? Of course not. Plenty of business opportunities came his way and his emotions were never involved. But this was different and it was because of Jess. He felt the sudden hardening of his groin. Because didn't her involvement guarantee the kind of satisfaction which went way beyond mere profit and loss?

'I heard the company was struggling because the management had become lazy, and I realised that I could turn it around. Take a famous brand and bring it bang up to date and you can't fail.' He smiled. 'And you know what they say…buy weak, sell strong.'

She was looking at him in faint surprise, as if she hadn't expected the slick soundbites of the professional negotiator to come from his lips. He felt the flicker of anger. *Because deep down she still thinks of you as a thug. A wall of muscle, without a life of your own or a brain you might be capable of using.*

'But of course your connection to the company made the prospect irresistible,' he said softly. 'Because I wanted to see you again.'

To see whether his desire for her had diminished. Whether the sight of her cool face would leave him cold. He glanced at her untouched plate and his gaze moved upwards. He saw the way the candlelight flickered over her neat breasts and suddenly he was overcome by a wave of lust so powerful that if he had been standing up, it might have knocked him off his feet. Because surprise, surprise, he thought bitterly, it hadn't left him—his desire hadn't left him at all. If anything, it had only increased—as if the years in between had only sharpened his sensual hunger. Right now it was consuming him like a newly lit fire and when he looked at those cool, parted lips he wanted to lean across the table and crush them beneath his. To slide his hand beneath her dull little dress. To move his fingers against her heated flesh. To bring her to a disbelieving orgasm and then have her suck him sweetly to his own.

His mouth hardened.

So what was he planning to do about it?

'You're not eating, Jess,' he said and he could hear how husky his voice sounded. He wondered if she was aware how heavy his groin felt, hidden by the snowy drapery of the tablecloth.

'Neither are you.' She pushed her plate away and nodded her head, as if she'd come to some kind of decision. 'And I'm not surprised. This meal was a bad idea. Just because we're going to work together doesn't mean we have to eat together. I'm going back to my room. I'll order something from Room Service.'

'I'll get the check and come with you.'

'No, honestly. You don't have to.' She licked her lips and gave a forced kind of smile. 'In fact, I'd much rather you didn't.'

'I insist.'

His silky determination silenced her and Jessica watched as he summoned the waiter and signed the check. She wondered if he cared how their behaviour must look to other people. Did the waiter consider it odd? Two people barely touching the amazing food or spectacular wine which had been placed before them. Two people sitting opposite one another, their bodies stiff and tense, looking as if they were engaged in some silent battle when in reality they were trying to ignore the sexual hunger still burning between them. She was aware of people watching as they weaved their way through the tables. The velvet-lined doors swung softly closed behind them, blotting out the faint chatter and low strains of music—and Jessica psyched herself up to say a dignified goodnight.

'Thanks, Loukas.'

'There's nothing to thank me for. I'll see you to your room.'

'But—'

He cut across her objection before she'd had a chance to voice it. 'Again, I insist.'

What else would he try to insist on? she wondered desperately as the elevator doors slid together, shutting out the rest of the world.

She tried to drag her gaze away from the chiselled perfection of his face. The elevator felt claustrophobic. Worse than that—it felt dangerous. There was no giant desk or restaurant table between them now, only a limited space so that he felt much too close, yet much too far. She could practically feel the heat radiating from his powerful body and the air seemed full of the scent which was so uniquely Loukas. She closed her eyes and breathed it in. A hint of citrus cut with spice, and underpinned with a raw and potent masculinity which took her straight back to the past. It filled her lungs, reminding her of all the pleasure he'd brought her. Reminding her of his hard kisses and soft kisses and all the in-between kisses. Of how he used to thrust so deep inside her. The first time, when it had hurt. And the second time, when it had felt as if she'd gone to heaven.

Could he hear the increased breathing, no matter how hard she tried to control it? Probably. His sense of hearing was acute—just like all his other senses. It was one of the things which had made him such a good bodyguard, as well as being such an amazing lover.

And suddenly Jessica found herself resenting the fact that he hadn't so much as touched her. He hadn't even done what anyone else in his position would have done—given her a cool kiss on either cheek when she'd walked into his office. No matter what he was feeling inside, that would have been the civilised thing to do.

But Loukas wasn't civilised, was he? Beneath the exquisite suit and unmistakable veneer of wealth, he was still the same man he'd always been. Basic and primeval and oozing testosterone. But he wasn't acting on it. He wasn't acting out her vivid fantasy of playing the primitive male and pinning her up against the wall and just *taking* her, as he'd done so often in the past.

Did he guess what she was feeling—or wanting? Was that why he was looking at her with that infuriating half-smile on his lips, which was completely at odds with the hunger which had begun to spark like dark fire in the depths of that burning gaze?

She found herself praying they would reach her floor soon, yet part of her never wanted to get there. She wanted to stay here, trapped in this small moving box with him—just the two of them—until one of them cracked.

Did she give herself away?

Was there some small movement which indicated the struggle she was having with herself? She wondered if she'd wriggled slightly or whether something about her posture had indicated that her breath felt as if it were trapped in the upper part of her throat.

'Oh,' he said slowly, his words suddenly shattering the fraught silence, as if she had just said something which required an answer. 'It's like that, is it?'

And he reached out to cup her chin with his hand, drawing his thumb almost lazily over lips which had begun to tremble uncontrollably. The mere touch of him was electrifying, the effect of it so profound that her head jerked, like a puppet on a string. Jessica's heart began to pound as he slipped the thumb inside her mouth and she couldn't seem to stop him from doing it, even if she'd wanted to. Pavlov's dog, she thought helplessly, aware that he was watching her, still with that infuriating half-smile on his face.

Her eyes had fluttered to a close as her lips closed round the thumb, and she wondered if that was to avoid the mockery in his eyes or because it meant she could pretend. Pretend that this was a normal interaction between a man and a woman, instead of one tainted with bitterness and regret. She felt him move the thumb very slightly—in and out, in and out—demonstrating a provocative mimicry of sex. *Kiss me,* she prayed silently as she sucked. Take some of this aching away and *just kiss me*.

'Open your eyes, Jess.'

Reluctantly, her lashes fluttered open and she found herself meeting the hardness of his piercing black gaze.

'Do you want me to kiss you?' he questioned softly as he withdrew the thumb so slowly that she almost groaned.

Had he read her mind, or had she said the words out loud without realising? Reluctantly, she nodded her head in silent acquiescence.

'Then ask me. Ask me nicely and I'll consider it.'

The corresponding rush of resentment gave her a last-minute reprieve and she glared at him. You don't have to do this, she told herself. You don't have to do what he says. 'Don't play games with me, Loukas.'

'I thought games were your speciality.'

'Go to hell.'

And then he *did* kiss her, laughing a little as he pulled her against him—his hard body driving every objection clean from her mind. All she could think about was how strong he was, and how good it felt to be back in his arms. Within the circle of his powerful embrace she felt warm, like an ice cube which had started to melt. She felt *safe*. But that didn't last long… And maybe that was the wrong description, because how could she possibly feel safe when his hands were sliding down over her breasts like that and making her moan with pleasure? It felt the opposite of safe when her nipples were thrusting against her dress and aching for him to bare them.

The lift pinged to a halt and Jessica felt the punch of frustration as Loukas dragged his mouth away from hers. His gaze was smoky, his expression suggesting he'd been as blown away by that kiss as she had. But his look of sensual surrender quickly cleared and was replaced by a cold-eyed assessment. For a minute she thought he was about to hit the button to send them back down the way they'd come—as if their evening would be spent riding an elevator which represented a private and no-threat world where none of the normal rules applied.

But she was wrong. He kept his finger firmly on the *doors open* button as his black gaze sizzled over her.

'So,' he said.

'So,' she repeated, more to gain time than anything else.

'Aren't you going to invite me inside?' he questioned.

Every fibre of her being was screaming at her to say yes. To open the door and do what she wanted to do more than she could remember wanting anything. She knew exactly what would happen. The look on his face told her that it would be quick. He would rip at her clothing. Push aside the damp panel of her panties with impatient fingers. She could almost *hear* the rasp of his zip as she pictured him freeing himself. Her fingers were itching to reacquaint themselves with that silken, steely shaft—to rub it up and down until he began to groan…

Blood rushed through her veins as she thought of that first intimate touch just before he entered her—the moist tip of him pressing against her—and she could have wept with longing and frustration. Would he be able to tell that there had been no lover since him? That he had been the one and only man she'd ever been intimate with? Would he laugh in disbelief if he knew, or would it simply make him gloat with insufferable pride? That he was still able to make her—the cool and contained Jessica Cartwright—into someone she barely recognised.

He had offered her the job and was now making it very clear that he wanted her. For a man with Loukas's reasoning, one would automatically follow the other. Payback time. And would that be such a terrible thing? If she had sex with him again it might make her look at things more rationally. Reassure herself that she'd built him up in her mind because she'd been young and impressionable. And this was a modern world, wasn't it? She should be able to sleep with whom she pleased.

She opened her mouth to say yes, but something stopped her—and that something was the look in his eyes. Was that *triumph* she could read there?

Some of the heat left her blood. She thought about how she'd feel in the morning if she woke up and found him beside her. Would she be able to deal with the aftermath of such a rash act? She doubted it. Because intimacy terrified her. It brought with it hurt, and pain. And surely only a fool would do something in the knowledge that it was going to bring them pain.

She shook her head. 'No, Loukas,' she said. 'I'm not.'

He bent his head forward, as if he didn't believe her, as if he could change her mind by shortening the physical distance between them. His breath was warm against her face.

'Are you sure?' he whispered.

It took every bit of will power she possessed to step back and shake her head, but will power was something she was good at. It was will power which had made her stand outside in all weathers, smashing ball after ball over the net while her father shouted at her. Will power which had dragged her out of bed on those cold winter mornings while the rest of her schoolfriends had snuggled beneath the duvet while their mothers made toast.

'Quite sure,' she answered. 'I'm going to bed. Alone. Goodnight.'

The faint flare of surprise she saw in his eyes gave her no real pleasure. It didn't cancel out the ache in her body or the yearning in her heart. Stepping inside her suite, she shut the door on his hard and beautiful face and resisted the desire to smash her fist against the wall.

CHAPTER FIVE

FRUSTRATION WAS NEVER a good feeling to wake up to, but Jessica supposed it was preferable to regret.

Standing beneath the pounding jets of the shower, she scrubbed furiously at her skin, as if doing that would wash the Greek from her memory, but nothing could shift the annoying thoughts going round and round inside her head. Had she been crazy not to invite Loukas into her suite, to kill the fantasy of her ex-lover once and for all? To make her realise that she'd been building him up into some kind of god for all these years, when in reality he was a mere mortal?

She reminded herself of the evening they'd shared. He had shown her no real affection, had he? He had taken her to dinner, then made a cold-blooded move on her afterwards. He had made her feel more like a potential conquest than an object of desire. Was she so desperate for sex that she was regretting not having settled for *that*? No, she was not. She needed to keep her wits about her and she needed to stay in control.

Pulling on a pair of linen trousers, she buttoned up her shirt and twisted her hair into a bun and was just clipping pearl studs into her ears when the phone beside the bed shattered the silence. She hesitated for a moment before picking up the handset. 'Yes?'

'Sleep well?'

The deep voice washed over her like dark honey. It made staying in control seem like the hardest thing in the world.

'Like a log,' she lied. 'Did you?'

'No, not really.' His voice dipped. 'I kept being woken up by the most erotic dreams imaginable and they all seemed to involve you. I blame you for my disturbed night, Jess.'

'Because you didn't get what you wanted?'

Loukas didn't answer. If only it were as simple as that. If only his frustration could be put down to the fact that she'd stopped him making love to her—but it wasn't that simple. It was starting to feel *complicated* and he didn't do complicated. Why had it become so important to possess her again, and why was she so determined to fight him?

He knew she wanted him—she'd made that very clear—and yet she had resisted. He wondered if she revelled in the power it gave her—to tap into that icy self-control which she pulled out just when you were least expecting it. She had fallen apart in his arms the moment he'd touched her, and yet still she had said no.

His mouth hardened. He was aware that he had the double standards of many men to whom sex had always come easily, but his attitudes had been reinforced by the unhappiness of his childhood and the things he had witnessed. Those things had soured him towards the opposite sex and the women he had met subsequently had done little to help modify his prejudices.

But Jess was different. She had always been different. Not just because she was streamlined and blonde, when his taste had always tended towards fleshy brunettes. She was the one woman who had walked away from him. The one he had never been able to work out. She had that indefinable something called *class*, which no amount of money could ever buy. It had been her aloofness which had first drawn him to her—something he'd never come into contact with before. That sense of physical and emotional distance had fascinated him and so had she. She was the first woman he'd ever had to woo. The first—and only—woman he'd ever bought flowers for. Had she secretly laughed at his cheap little offering—when sophisticated bouquets had awaited her when she walked off the tennis court? He'd often wondered whether it had been her secret fantasy to take someone like him as her first lover. Someone as unlike her as possible. Someone who knew what it was all about, but who could safely be discarded afterwards. Her *piece of rough*. Had he served his purpose by deflowering her and introducing her to pleasure?

He considered the options which lay open to him. He could walk away now. Leave the new advertising campaign in the hands of the experts, and keep his own input to the bare minimum. Or he could pay her off with an overinflated sum, since money was the reason she was here. He could find a fresher, newer model, with none of the baggage which Jessica Cartwright carried. And he could easily find himself another lover. One who would not cold-bloodedly shut the door in his face, but who would welcome him with open arms and open legs.

But he had not finished with her. Not yet. His list was not yet completed. He had met his brother. He had dealt with his mother's betrayal and uncovered all the dark secrets she had left behind. He had built up a fortune beyond his wildest dreams. He had made some of his peace with the world, so that only Jessica remained—and he needed her. He needed to take his fill of her, because only then would he be free of her and able to walk away.

'Maybe I didn't get what I wanted last night, *koukla mou*,' he said softly, 'but I always get there in the end.'

He heard her suck in a deep breath.

'What happened between us last night. You must realise that it changes everything.'

He affected innocence. 'How?'

There was a moment of silence. He could hear her searching for words. He wondered if she would try to hide behind those polite little platitudes which didn't mean a thing.

'I can't possibly work alongside you now!'

'Don't make such a big deal out of it, Jess,' he said. 'Our bodies are programmed to react towards each other that way. You want me and I want you. We've always had chemistry. Big deal. We're both grown-ups and neither of us are in relationships—at least, I'm not and I'm assuming you aren't either.'

'Isn't that something you should have asked me before you leapt on me in the elevator?'

'I don't know if I would describe it as *leaping*,' he commented drily. 'And I was assuming you might have put up some kind of objection had that been the case.'

'How do you manage to twist everything I say?'

'Is that what I am doing, *koukla mou*?' he questioned innocently.

'You know you are.'

'So why don't we put down what happened to curiosity and leave it at that? The advertising team want to meet you at their offices,' he added. 'My car will be outside your hotel at eleven.'

Jessica was left staring at the phone as he did that frustrating thing of ringing off before she felt the conversation was finished. Though really, what was there left to say? She ordered breakfast from Room Service, nibbling half-heartedly on a piece of wholemeal toast, and drank two cups of coffee strong enough to re-vive her. But when she went down to the front of the hotel just after eleven, it was to find Loukas sitting in the back of a car parked directly outside, reading through a large sheaf of documents.

'Oh, it's you,' she said as he glanced up, and was caught in his ebony gaze. Her heart gave a punch of excitement she didn't *want* to feel, but was it really so surprising that she was reacting to him? Last time she'd seen him he'd had his tongue down her throat and she had been in danger of dissolving beneath his touch. Was he remembering that, too? Was that why his eyes were gleaming with inky provocation and his lips had curved into a mocking smile?

'Yes, Jess. It's me.'

She swallowed as the driver shut the door behind her. 'I wasn't expecting to find you here.'

'But hoping you might?'

'You're…'

'I'm what, Jess?'

She shook her head. 'It doesn't matter.'

'Oh, come on,' he taunted softly. 'Why hide behind that frozen expression you're so fond of—why not come out and say just what you're thinking for once?'

She stared at him, her heart beating very fast, and suddenly she thought, What the heck? Why *shouldn't* he know how she felt about him? She wasn't on a tennis court now and he wasn't her opponent. Well, he *was*, but not in the traditional sense. What did it matter if she was honest with him—the world wouldn't stop turning if she told him the truth, would it? But it wasn't easy to voice her emotions, when she'd been drilled to keep them hidden away ever since she could remember. Wasn't that why sex with him had been so wonderful—and so scary—because it had knocked all those barriers down, and for a little while had made her feel free? 'Actually, you're the last person I wanted to see.'

'Liar,' he said softly. 'Stop pretending—most of all to yourself. Your body language gave you away the moment you saw me again. Even you can't disguise the darkening of your eyes or the unmistakable tightening of those delicious breasts.'

'How come you're even *here*?' she said crossly as the car pulled away from the kerb.

He laughed. 'I live here.'

'You live in a hotel?'

'Why not?'

'Because…because a hotel is somewhere you stay. It's not a real home.'

'For some people it is.'

Loukas stared out of the window as the streets of London passed them by. Would it shock her to discover that he'd never really had a home of his own, just a series of places in which to stay? He remembered the too-thin curtain at one end of the room, and the saving grace of the cotton-wool plugs which he'd crammed into his ears and which had blotted out most of the sounds. 'Actually, it's ideal for all my needs,' he said. 'It's big, it's central and there are several award-winning restaurants just minutes away from my suite. I send out for what I want. My car gets valet parked and there is effective security on the door. What's not to like?'

'But don't you like having all your own things around you?'

He turned back to look at her. 'What things?'

She shrugged. 'Oh, you know. Pictures. Ornaments. Photos.'

'The clutter of the past?' He smiled. 'No. I'm not a big fan of possessions. I try to live by the maxim that you should always be able to walk away, with a single suitcase and your passport.'

She frowned. 'But what about the future? Do you plan to live in a hotel for ever—is that what you want?'

'There is no future,' he said softly. 'There is only what we have right now and right now all I want to do is kiss you, but unfortunately there isn't time.' He reached for his jacket. 'We're here.'

Heart pounding, Jessica stared out of the car window. 'Here?'

'Zeitgeist. The best advertising agency in London.'

She looked up at the cathedral-high dimensions as they entered the modern building, forcing herself to concentrate on her surroundings instead of focusing on how much she had *wanted* him to kiss her back then. 'Tell me why we're here?'

'Gabe and his team would like to show you a mock-up for the new campaign. They've been in pre-production for weeks and want to present you with your brief.'

They were ushered into a huge room filled with a confusing amount of people. She was introduced to Patti, the stylist—a spiky-haired blonde in a bright green mini-dress and a pair of chunky boots who was swishing through a rail of clothes. The long-haired art director was peering at photos of a woman standing on a gondola—a gondola!—who looked suspiciously like her. And when she looked a bit closer she could see that it was indeed her—with her head superimposed onto the body of some sleek model wearing a series of revealing evening dresses, set off with dazzling displays of diamonds.

There was a dynamism in the air which was almost palpable and nothing like the rather slow pace of the advertising agency Lulu had employed before. In fact, it was all a bit of a whirlwind experience, made all the more intense by Loukas at her side—warm and vibrant, and impossible to ignore. He took her over to the far side of the studio to meet Gabe Steel, the agency's owner—a striking man with dark golden hair and steely grey eyes.

'When Loukas explained that he wanted a complete change of image for the Lulu brand,' Gabe was saying, 'I could see it was a change which was long overdue. So we're ditching the Grace Kelly look and going for something more modern. We've had a lot of fun putting these new ideas together, Jessica—and I think you're going to like them. I showed them to my wife last night and she certainly did.' He smiled. 'So why don't you sit down and you can see what we have in mind?'

Jessica sat down on a chair which had clearly been chosen more for style than comfort and watched as the art director and Patti whipped through a series of photos, showcasing different pieces of jewellery.

'We're taking out a two-page spread in one of the broadsheets just in time for Valentine's Day,' explained Gabe, 'which only gives us a few weeks to play with.'

'Valentine's Day?' repeated Jessica, thinking that no other date could have rubbed in her single status quite so effectively.

'Sure. It's one of the jewellery business's most profitable times of the year—and Lulu needs to capitalise on that in a way it has failed to do before. The young girls who used to buy the wristwatch are all grown up now, and we want to show the world that you've grown up, too. We want to show that the new Jessica is definitely not a girl any more. And she won't be wearing a waterproof wristwatch, she'll be wearing jewels—preferably some which have been bought for her by a man.'

'My jewels,' interjected Loukas softly.

Jessica thought how weird it was to hear herself being spoken about in the third person. She stared nervously at the photos. Surely they weren't expecting her to wear clothes like *those*—with half her breasts on show, or a long dress slashed all the way up the way up her thigh?

'The shoot is booked to take place in Venice, as you can see from the mock-ups,' Gabe continued. 'It's the most romantic city in the world and a perfect setting for the kind of look we're aiming for. In winter it's moody and atmospheric, which is why we'll be shooting in black and white with the iconic Lulu pink as the only colour.' He smiled at her. 'The team are going out first to set up the locations and I gather you and Loukas are flying out separately.'

Every face in the room turned to look at her, but all Jessica could see was the gleam of Loukas's black eyes and the faint curve of his mocking smile. Since when had they been travelling out *separately* and why hadn't anyone bothered to tell her about it? She didn't think she'd ever shouted at anyone in her life but right then Jessica wanted to stand up and yell that she didn't want to go *anywhere* with the arrogant Greek—least of all to a city famed for romance, to advertise a campaign which was *all* about romance.

She wanted to be back in Cornwall, far away from him and the uncomfortable way he was making her feel. She had been fine before he'd come back into her life. Things might have been predictable, but at least they had felt *safe*. She hadn't been racked with longing, or regret. She hadn't started thinking about the fact that they'd never even spent a whole night together.

Did she *really* have to take this job—with all the complications which accompanied it? Again, she thought about selling up and buying a cheaper apartment away from the sea.

But then her half-sister's face drifted into her mind and she felt the sharp stab of her conscience. She thought of Hannah sobbing in her arms following the terrible avalanche which had killed her parents. Things had been bad enough when they'd been forced to sell the big house, but they had chosen the new one *together*, and Hannah loved her current home. It was her home, too, and what right did Jessica have to deprive her of that security, just because being around Loukas bothered her more than it should have done?

She didn't have to sleep with him, no matter how much she wanted him. And there was nothing to stop her making it clear to him that it wasn't going to happen. A new sense of determination filled her, because hadn't she come through far worse than having to resist a man like him?

So she gave Gabe a smile—the same smile she always used when people asked if she missed playing tennis. A very useful smile to have in her repertoire. It was bright and convincing.

And it didn't mean a thing.

'I can't wait,' she said.

CHAPTER SIX

LOUKAS WATCHED AS Jessica stood in the gondola, her new, shorter hair being ruffled by the wind. Her face was pale, her eyes looked huge, and the tension surrounding her was almost palpable. Not for the first time that day, he clenched his fists with frustration, because this had been his idea and on paper it had seemed like an outstanding one. All the boxes had been ticked. She wore a tight-fitting, corseted black ballgown which hugged her slender body and emphasised her neat little breasts. Long black satin gloves came up to her elbow and a waterfall of diamonds glittered against her breasts.

It should have been perfect. Jessica Cartwright looking exactly as the team at Zeitgeist had wanted her to look. Sleek and grown-up and very, very sexy.

Yet she stood there like a waxwork. Her

eyes seemed empty and her expression blank. Even her smile looked as if it had been plastered on.

He shook his head in disbelief as he thought back to the way she'd been in his arms the other night, when he'd kissed her in the elevator. She had been fire that night, not ice—but where was all that fire now?

His eyes bored into hers.

There was nothing left but embers.

From her precarious position in the Grand Canal, Jessica met Loukas's stony black gaze, which was boring into her from the side of the water. None of the crew were happy—she could tell. Not one of them, but especially not Loukas, who seemed to have been glaring at her since the shoot had got underway. The chill Venetian wind whipped around her as she tried to keep her balance, which wasn't easy when she was standing on a bobbing gondola.

She felt cold—inside and out. Around her neck hung a priceless dazzle of blue-white diamonds which shone like a beacon in the gloom of the winter day. Her newly bare neck—shorn back in London of its protective curtain of long hair—was now completely exposed to the wintry Venetian elements. Strands of the sleek new style fluttered around her chin and were starting to stick to her lip-gloss. And even though Patti the stylist stood next to her—poised with a hairbrush and a big cashmere wrap—that didn't stop Jessica from feeling ridiculously underdressed. These photos were light years away from the demure and sporty shots she usually did for the store and she felt *stupid*. No. She felt exposed.

And vulnerable.

Her eyelashes were laden down with more mascara than she'd ever worn before and consequently the smoky make-up they'd been aiming for looked as if someone had given her two black eyes. The glossy, cyclamen-pink lipstick, intended to echo the colour of the brand's iconic packaging, gave her an almost clown-like appearance. And the dress. Oh, the dress. She didn't even want to get started on the dress. It was everything she wasn't—vampy and revealing. Ebony satin fitted so closely on the bodice that she could barely breathe and cut so low that her cleavage was now an unflattering sea of goosebumps. Beneath the swish of the full skirt her knees were knocking together with a mixture of nerves and embarrassment. Because even though the city was relatively quiet in February, the odd tourist had stopped to take her photo and she hated it.

She hated trying to look *sexy and sophisticated*, which was the look the art director had told her he wanted—since she felt neither. She felt like a fraud—and wouldn't they all laugh themselves silly if they discovered that she hadn't made love to a man in eight long years?

Of course, having Loukas standing watching her wasn't helping. In fact, it was making everything a whole lot worse. Against the misty grey and white of the Venetian backdrop, the Greek stood out like a dark spectre on the bank of the canal. The light from the water caught him in its silvery gleam and the city's sense of the hidden and the deep seemed to reflect back his own unknowable personality. Two burly security guards flanked him, their eyes fixed on the fortune in gems which shimmered against her skin.

The art director looked at his watch and frowned. 'Okay, we're losing the light. Let's call it a day, shall we? Same time tomorrow, people.'

As some of the crew sprang forward to help her from the gondola, Jessica could see the art director muttering something to Loukas, who was nodding his head in thoughtful agreement. His black gaze held hers for a moment and she felt the skitter of unwanted desire whispering over her skin. Why was he even here? Why didn't he go back to London and leave her alone? Surely she might be able to come up with what they wanted if he weren't standing there, like a fire-breathing dragon, making her feel inadequate in all kinds of ways. Holding the voluminous folds of the black satin skirt of her dress, she stepped onto the bank and was handed the cashmere shawl.

'We're going to St Mark's Square for coffee, though maybe you deserve a brandy after all that,' said Patti, rubbing her hands together before putting them over her mouth and blowing on them. 'Fancy coming along once you've taken your necklace off and changed?'

'Not right now. I'm going to take Jess back to the hotel,' came a dark and silky voice from behind her.

Jessica glanced round to see Loukas walking towards her, like a character who had just stepped from an oil painting. His dark cashmere overcoat matched the dark gleam of his hair and today he seemed devoid of all colour. Today, he was all black. The hard-edged smile he glimmered at her set off faint warning bells, though she wasn't sure why.

'Because she looks frozen,' he added deliberately.

Yes, she was frozen, but, although her skin felt like ice, her blood grew heated when his fingers brushed against her neck as he unclipped the heavy diamonds and handed them over to the waiting security guard. She felt lighter once the jewels had been removed and she wrapped the shawl tightly around herself, trying to hide herself from Loukas's searching gaze. But nothing could protect her from the way he was making her feel, as self-conscious beneath that piercing stare as she had been during their journey out here.

They had taken a scheduled flight from London, which had been just about tolerable, because at least Loukas had been working while Jessica attempted to read a book. But when they had arrived and their waiting water taxi had taken them towards the city, she'd felt herself unwillingly caught up in the romance of the moment, no matter how hard she tried to fight it.

She had felt as if she were in a film as the sleek craft sped through the choppy grey waters, leaving a trail of white plume behind them, and the iconic skyline of cities, churches and domes loomed up ahead of them. She had failed to conceal her gasp of pleasure as they'd entered the Grand Canal and Loukas had turned to her and smiled. A complicit smile edged with danger and, yes, with promise.

And Jessica had shivered just as she was shivering now.

'Let's walk back to the hotel,' he said as the crew began to disperse.

Picking up the heavy skirt to prevent it from dragging on the damp bank, she looked at him. 'You really think I can walk back to the hotel wearing this?'

'You don't imagine that women in ages past had to struggle with dresses similar to that?' he mused. 'Think of the famous masked ball they hold here every February. And you'll be warmer if we walk. Come on. It isn't far.'

'Okay,' she said, and pulled the cashmere closer.

She stuck close to his side as they began to weave their way through the narrow streets, past shop windows filled with leather books and exquisite glassware and over tiny, echoing bridges. It was like being in the centre of an ancient maze and it wasn't long before Jessica had completely lost her bearings. 'You seem to know exactly where you're going,' she said.

'Unless you think I'm planning to get you lost in Venice, never to be seen again?'

She looked up at him and her heart gave a funny kind of thud. 'Are you?'

He laughed. 'Tempting, but no. Look. We're here.'

It was with something almost like disappointment that Jessica glanced up to see their hotel ahead of them, with light spilling out from the elegant porticoed entrance. Heads turned as they walked into the palm-filled foyer and she guessed that they must make a bizarre couple with her in the flowing ball-gown and Loukas in his black cashmere coat. She could feel the swish of her dress brushing over the marble floor and felt her cheeks grow pink when the pianist broke into a version of 'Isn't She Lovely?' and a group of businessmen started clapping and cheering as she passed them by. She wanted to dive into the elevator but her suite was on the first floor and the sweeping staircase seemed the most sensible option for getting there. But the voluminous skirt of her dress took some manoeuvring and she was out of breath by the time she got to the top.

'Not quite as fit as you used to be?' Loukas said, his black eyes glinting.

'Obviously not, since I'm not playing competitive tennis any more, but I'm fit enough. I'm just not used to dragging this amount of material around with me.'

There was a pause as they reached her door and she fumbled with her key card to open it.

'So, are you going to have dinner with me tonight?' he asked.

She shook her head. 'Thanks for the offer, but I'm going to have a bath and try to get warm again. My hands feel like ice.' She hesitated as she looked up into his face and then swallowed. 'They didn't like what I did today, did they? I could tell.'

He shrugged. 'It was all new to you. You're used to being brisk and breezy, to wearing casual clothes and looking sporty—and suddenly you're expected to start behaving like a vamp. You're operating outside your comfort zone, Jess, but don't worry. You'll get it right tomorrow.'

'And if I don't?'

His eyes glinted again. 'We'll just have to make sure you do.' He brushed a reflective finger down over her spine. 'Have you thought how you're planning to get out of this dress? Unless you're something of a contortionist you might have something of a problem, since it has about a hundred hooks.'

Jessica was trying not to react to the brush of his finger and she cursed the restrictive fastenings intended to give her an hourglass shape. She knew what he was suggesting but the thought of him helping her undress seemed all wrong. Yet what else was she going to do? Patti and the crew were in some unknown bar in an unknown city, and, short of waiting for them to return, she certainly couldn't undo it herself.

'Would you mind?' she said casually, as if it didn't bother her one way or the other.

'No, I don't mind,' he said, just as casually, as he followed her into the suite.

It was the most beautiful place she had ever stayed in, but Jessica barely noticed the carved furniture or the beautifully restored antique piano which stood beneath a huge chandelier. Even the stunning view over the Grand Canal and the magnificent dome of the Salute church couldn't distract her from the thought that Loukas was here, in her hotel room.

'Aren't you going to turn around and look at me, Jess?' he questioned softly.

She cleared her throat, wondering if he could hear her nervousness. 'You're supposed to be undoing my dress,' she said. 'And you can't do that unless I have my back to you.'

There was a split second of a pause. She thought she heard him give a soft laugh as he unclipped the first hook, and then the second. She wanted to tell him to hurry up and yet she wanted him to take all the time in the world. She could feel the rush of air to her back as he loosened the gown and she closed her eyes as another hook was liberated. Was this how women used to feel in the days before they were free to wear short dresses and trousers, or go without a bra? A sense of being completely within a man's power as he slowly undressed her?

Her breath caught in her throat because now there was a contrast between the air which had initially cooled her skin being replaced by the unmistakable warmth of a breath. Her eyelashes fluttered. Was he…was he breathing against her bare back?

Yes, he was.

It felt like the most intimate thing imaginable. She swallowed, because now his lips were pressing against the skin and he was actually *kissing* her there.

Her eyes closed. She knew she ought to say something but every nerve in her body was telling her not to break the spell. Because this was anonymous, wasn't it? It was pleasurable and anonymous, and she didn't have to think. She didn't have to remember that this was Loukas and that there was bad history between them. She didn't have to look into those gleaming black eyes or see triumph curving his lips into a mocking smile. All she was conscious of was the feel of his lips brushing against her and the hot prickling of her breasts in response.

The dress had slid down to her hips and his hands were moving to skim their curves as if he was rediscovering them. Luxuriantly, he spread his fingers over the flesh and she thought she heard him give a sigh of pleasure. She swallowed, but still she didn't say anything, because it was easier to play dumb. To want it to continue yet not be seen to be encouraging it. Her heart began to beat even faster because now he had started brushing his fingers over her lacy thong and with that came a wave of lust so strong that it washed away the residual grains of her conscience.

'Mmm,' he said as the dress fell to the ground, pooling around her ankles and leaving her legs completely bare. He was kissing her neck and his fingers were hooking into her panties and she felt a molten rush of heat.

She knew she should stop him. But she couldn't. She just *couldn't*. It had been so long since she had done this and she was cold. So cold. And Loukas was making her feel warm. Warmer than she'd felt in a long time.

His fingers had moved from her hip and were now inside her panties, alighting on her heated flesh with a familiarity which seemed as poignant as it was exciting.

'It's been a long time,' he said almost reflectively, drifting a fingertip across the engorged bud.

Jessica's body jerked with pleasure. She wanted to say something—anything—as if to reassure herself that she was still there and that it was all real. But the words simply wouldn't come. His touch had robbed her of the power to speak. Her breath had dried in her throat and all she could think about was the hunger building up inside her and dominating her whole world. Her thighs seemed to be parting of their own accord and she felt the warmth of his breath as he smiled against her neck.

'You are very wet, *koukla mou*,' he murmured.

She swallowed as her eyes closed. 'Yes.'

'Wet for me?'

'Y-yes.'

'Have you been imagining me touching you here?'

'Yes!'

'And...*here*?'

'God, yes.' Jessica gasped, even though his words seemed to contradict his actions. Because what he was saying was provocative, but strangely cold. He was objectifying her, she realised with a brief rush of horror and she tried to pull away. To end it while she still could. But by then it was too late because she was starting to come and he was giving a low laugh of triumph as he swivelled her round to cover her mouth with his, his hand still cupping her flesh while his kiss drowned out her broken cry of surrender.

His tongue was in her mouth as she pulsated

helplessly around his finger and the combination of that double invasion only increased her pleasure, until she thought she might have slid to the ground, if he hadn't been holding onto her so tightly. Time passed in a slow, throbbing haze before her eyelids fluttered open to find Loukas watching her, still with that faintly triumphant smile on his face. Slowly, he withdrew his finger and she noted that it wasn't quite steady.

'Jess,' he said and picked her up and carried her into the bedroom to lie her down on the bed.

'Loukas,' she whispered, and the tip of her tongue came out to slide over her parted lips.

Loukas felt the savage beat of his heart as he looked at her glistening mouth and his erection was so hard that it took him a moment or two before he was able to move. He wanted to tear off his clothes and just *take* her. But not yet. Not until he was in control of his feelings. Until he was certain that he was in no danger of being trapped by the powerful spell she had always been able to weave around him.

He tried to study her objectively as he shrugged off his overcoat and hung it over the back of a chair, then went back towards the bed on which she lay. Strange that she should have been so cold and uptight in front of the camera today and yet had fallen apart the moment he'd touched her. But hadn't that always been her way? He gave a bitter smile. The only time he'd ever been able to penetrate her haughty exterior—in more ways than one— was when she was naked and writhing beneath him. Because outside the bedroom, or the sitting room, or the car—or wherever else they happened to have been doing it—she had always been the very definition of cool.

But not now.

Her eyes were smoky, her face flushed with satisfaction and her thighs parted in such open invitation that he was almost tempted to bury his head between them and lick her. He thought how at home she looked, lying back against the brocade covering the ornate four-poster bed. But of course, she was. This place was classy and luxurious; it was the environment to which she was most suited. *The one in which he had never quite fitted.*

He reached out his hand and laid it over her left breast. He could feel her heart pounding beneath the lace of her provocative bra as he circled a thumb over the nipple which was peaking through the scarlet and black lace. 'You never used to wear such frivolous under-wear when I was with you, *koukla mou*,' he observed silkily. 'So what happened? Did the men who followed me demand that you dress to please—or have your tastes simply changed and evolved with time?'

Jessica opened her mouth to tell him that Patti had taken her shopping after they'd been to the hairdresser, explaining that the revealing gowns wouldn't tolerate anything except the briefest of bras, and that her panties should preferably match *to get her in the mood* for the shoot. Except that it hadn't worked out that way, had it? She had stood posing like a female ice cube in the dramatic and sexy dress and had only really come to life when Loukas had touched her.

She bit her lip. And how he had touched her. She had forgotten how exquisite an orgasm could feel when it was administered by the only man she had ever really cared about. She had forgotten how weak and powerless it could make you feel. As if all your strength had been sapped. It could make you vulnerable if you weren't careful, and she needed to be careful.

She shouldn't have allowed it to happen, but now that she had she wanted it continue. She had acted foolishly but maybe understandably—or at least, understandable to her. She was like someone who'd broken her diet by opening a packet of cookies. But why stop at one, when four would be much more satisfactory and make the sin worthwhile? She didn't want her enduring memory of sex with Loukas to be a one-sided, rather emotionless pleasuring. She wanted to make love to him properly. Hadn't she wanted that for years? She wanted to feel him inside her. Deep inside her. Filling her and heating her as nothing else could.

She reached up her hand and began to unbutton his shirt, determined to approach this as if they were equals. Because she wasn't some little virgin who'd just been seduced, and though she might lack his undoubted sexual experience, there was no reason for him to know that.

'Do you really want to talk about other men at a moment like this?' she questioned coolly, slipping free another button and rubbing her hand against his hair-roughened chest.

His mouth tightened as he leaned forward

and began to tug at the belt of his trousers. 'No,' he said. 'I don't. And soon you won't be able to, because I'm going to make you forget every other man you've had sex with. You won't be able to remember a single damned thing about them, because all you'll be able to think about is *me*.'

The arrogant boast shocked her but it thrilled her, too. Nearly as much as it thrilled her to see him peel off his clothes to reveal his body in all its honed olive splendour. It was as magnificent as it had ever been but suddenly Jessica gasped because there—zigzagging over the side of his torso like a fleshy fork of lightning—was a livid scarlet scar. Her fingers flew to her lips before reaching out to touch it, as tentatively as if it might still hurt. As if it might open up and begin to bleed all over the bed.

'What happened to you?' she whispered.

'Not now, Jess,' he growled.

'But—'

'I said, not now.' His hand slid between her thighs and began to move, effectively silencing all further questioning. 'Does that kind of detail please you?' he rasped. 'Does it turn you on to think that your rough, tough bodyguard has the mark of violence on his body?'

There was something in his tone she didn't understand—some dark note which lay just beneath the mockery—and Jessica was confused. But by then he was stroking her again and his mouth was on her breast, and she was growing so hot for him that she could barely wait for him to slide on the condom and position himself over her.

She was trembling as he made that first thrust and the sensation surpassed every fantasy she'd ever had about him. But to her surprise, he was trembling, too, and for several moments his big body stayed completely still, as if he didn't trust himself to move.

She wanted to whisper things to him. Soft, stupid things. She wanted to tell him that she wished she'd married him when he'd asked her. That she'd thrown away the best chance of happiness she'd ever had. But nobody could rewrite history—and didn't they say everything happened for a reason? Even if right now it was difficult to see what that reason could possibly be.

And then all the nagging thoughts were driven from her mind because her orgasm

was happening again. It built up into a cre-
scendo and sent her into total meltdown—and
the shuddered moan which echoed around the
room told her that so, too, had his.

CHAPTER SEVEN

THE ROOM WAS very quiet for what seemed like a long time and, when she spoke, Jessica's words seemed to splinter the peace. She turned onto her side and stared into the face of the man beside her.

'How did you get that scar?'

Loukas stirred and stretched. Completely comfortable in his nakedness, he raised his arms and extended his powerful legs in a movement which should have distracted her, but nothing could have distracted her right then. All Jessica could see was the livid mark zigzagging over his flesh.

'How?' she whispered again, when still he didn't answer.

His face became shuttered as he drifted a fingertip over her nipple and watched it wrinkle and harden. 'As a topic for pillow talk,' he drawled, 'it's not exactly up there with telling me how much you enjoyed your orgasm.'

Jessica didn't react. He made what had happened sound so *clinical*. But maybe for him it was. Did legions of women purr the morning afterwards and tell the dark and charismatic Greek how much they had enjoyed their orgasm? She scooped back her hair and peered at him. 'Was it in Paris?' she persisted.

'Was what in Paris?' He stopped stroking.

'You told me that you were…captured there.' She hesitated. His face was still shuttered, but she persisted. 'Was it back then?'

Loukas lay back, pillowing his ruffled head on his folded arms as the chandelier glittered fractured light on their bare skin. He sensed she wouldn't give up until she had an answer and something told him he was going to find it harder to silence Jess than he would the average lover. 'No, it wasn't then,' he said dismissively.

'So…when?'

He turned his head to look at her and frowned. 'Does it matter?'

'Of course it matters.' She gave a barely perceptible sigh. 'What is it with you, Loukas? You never talk about your past, and you never did. I was with you for months and ended up knowing almost nothing about you.'

He gave the flicker of a smile. 'You knew plenty.'

'I'm not talking about the way your body works.'

He gave a short laugh. She had grown up in a land of milk and honey, in a world light years away from his. He thought about the big house with the tennis court and the bright green lawns which swept down to the sea. About privilege and belonging and all the things he'd never had. 'What difference does it make to know about my past?'

'It might make me feel as if I wasn't in bed with a stranger,' she said quietly.

It wasn't the first time the accusation had been levelled at him, but, when Jess said it, it felt different. Come to think of it—everything about Jess felt different. 'I thought the anonymity aspect appealed to you,' he drawled. 'You certainly seemed turned on when you had your back to me earlier. For a minute I thought you might be pretending I was someone else.'

'Don't try to change the subject.'

'I'll do anything I please. Just because I've

made love to you doesn't give you the right to censor my speech, or to demand answers.'

She bit her lip. 'Is it such an awful story, then?'

'Yes.' He said the word without planning and it was like an overfilled balloon being popped by the prick of a needle. Like a bruise beneath your fingernail which only a white-hot lance would relieve. 'Yes,' he repeated. 'Awful gets pretty close to it.'

'Won't you tell me?'

His instinct was to distract her—either by making love to her again, or by heading off to take a shower. Because she wanted to talk about the old Loukas, and he had spent a long time forging a new Loukas, a man as hard as the diamonds which were at the core of his fortune and a success beyond his wildest dreams.

He had uncovered secrets he would have preferred to have left alone, and had hidden them away deep inside himself. But secrets left their mark, he was discovering—a dirty mark which left a stain if you didn't expose it to the sunshine and the air. He looked into Jess's cool features, but for once her face was showing the emotions she usually kept contained. He could see the concern shadowing her eyes. He could hear an anxious softness in her voice, and something made him start talking. 'How much do you know?'

She shrugged. 'Not a lot. That you were an only child and your mother brought you up in Athens, and that you never knew who your father was.'

Loukas twisted his mouth into a grim smile. How easily a whole life could be condensed into a single sentence—black and white, without a single shade of grey in between. 'Did I tell you that we were poor?'

'Not in so many words, but I...' Her words tailed off.

'You what, Jess?' he said silkily. 'You guessed?'

She nodded.

'How?'

'It doesn't matter.'

'Oh, but it does. I'm interested.'

Reluctantly, she shrugged. 'You just always seemed so...oh, I don't know...restless, I guess. Like a shark moving through the water. Like you were always looking for something.'

It startled him how accurate her words were and Loukas nodded. Because she was right. He *had* been looking for something—he just hadn't known what it was. And then, when he'd found it...

'We were dirt poor, my mother and I,' he said, wanting to ram home the fundamental differences between them. To shock her. To convince her—and him—that all they shared was a rare electricity in between the sheets. 'Sometimes I used to hang around at the backs of restaurants to see what food they were throwing away at the end of a day's trade, and I'd take it home...' Take it home and hang around outside until his mother had finished with whoever she was currently *entertaining*. He remembered the different men who had stumbled out, some of them trying to cuff him on the mouth, while others had pressed a few coins into his hand. But Loukas had never kept those coins. He'd put them in the poor box at the nearby church...unwilling to accept money which was *tainted*, no matter how hungry he'd been. 'Although I took what jobs I could, just as soon as I was old enough—running errands, sweeping restaurants, polishing cars—anything, really.'

'And your mother?' she questioned hesitantly. 'Did she work?'

'She didn't have time to work,' he said bitterly. 'She was too busy devoting herself to whoever her current love interest was. She always had to have a man around and a child like me was only ever going to get in the way. So for the most part, I was left to my own devices.'

'Oh, Loukas,' she breathed.

'I lived from hand to mouth,' he continued grimly. 'I worked at the ferry port in Piraeus as soon as I was old enough, until I'd saved up enough money to take myself off to a new life. I didn't go back to Greece for a long, long time. I did my own tour of Europe, only it was nothing like the ones you see advertised in the glossy brochures. I lived in the shadows of Paris. I learnt to box in the Ukraine, and for a while I won amateur fights all over the continent, until Dimitri Makarov asked me to be his bodyguard.'

'And that was when you met me,' she said slowly.

Loukas nodded slowly. Yes. That was when he'd met his fairy-tale princess, with her white skin and her blue eyes and the cutest little bottom he'd ever seen. Her coolness had fascinated him; she'd been restrained and cautious—nothing like his mother or all the women he'd subsequently been intimate with. She hadn't been predatory or coquettish. In fact she'd fought against an attraction which had been almost palpable. And hadn't the fact that his princess had presented him with her virginity been like a master stroke in capturing his heart as well as his body, culminating in that proud proposal of marriage which had been thrown back in his face? He gave a bitter laugh. What a fool he had been.

'Yes,' he said, with a note of finality. 'That was when I met you.'

'And did you ever…?' She drew in a deep breath and he saw the rise of her tiny breasts. 'Did you ever see your mother again?'

Loukas flinched, because it didn't matter what hurt and what pain she had caused him—she was still his mother.

'Only once,' he said flatly. 'I'd been sending her money for years, but I couldn't face returning. And then, when she was dying I went back to find her living in a…hovel.' His voice tailed off, before taking on a bitter note. 'In thrall to her latest boyfriend—a vulture who was systematically bleeding her dry of her dignity, as well as all the money I'd sent her. I remember how weak she was when she took my hand and told me that she *loved* this particular loser. And even though she'd been a notoriously bad picker of men all her life—this one was in a class of his own. He had neglected to give her any pain relief—he'd been too busy spending her money at the casino.'

'Was that when you got the scar?' she said slowly.

Loukas nodded, realising how alien this must all sound to someone like her. *'Neh,'* he drawled, the flicker of anger not far from the surface. He remembered being young and fit and prepared to fight fairly, but his mother's lover had not. He hadn't seen the glint of steel as the knife had come flashing down out of nowhere, and at first he hadn't even registered the strange, digging sensation in his flesh, which had heralded the eruption of blood. Loukas's voice shook with rage. 'The only good thing that came out of it was that he was arrested and jailed and no longer able to steal money from my mother. But by then it was too late anyway.'

'What do you mean?' she whispered.

'She died later that week, just as I was being discharged from hospital,' he said, his face twisted with pain. 'I found all her paperwork and I understood at last why she had never wanted to talk about my father.' He met the question in her eyes. 'Like I said, she was a bad picker of men and that my father was abusive to her came as no real surprise. But the most interesting thing was that I discovered I had a twin brother.'

She tipped her head back, her eyes huge. '*A twin brother?*'

He nodded. 'Alek had been brought up by my father—a very different kind of upbringing from mine. I had him tracked down and I met him in Paris.' It had been that meeting which had made Loukas decide to lay *all* of his ghosts to rest. To make him want to move on and live his life in a different way. And hadn't Jess been the most persistent ghost of them all—the one who had hovered on the periphery of his mind like some pale and interesting beauty?

'How...' her voice trembled '...how can you possibly have discovered that you have a twin? Why didn't your mother ever tell you?'

'Because my father was powerful,' he said. 'And she was running away from him. She couldn't physically—or financially—take two tiny babies, so she chose to leave Alek.'

'How? How did she choose?'

He shook his head. 'Doesn't matter how. She knew she could never go back and so she decided to cut out that part of her life completely. To pretend it had never happened.' He gave a short laugh. 'And if I'm being objective, I think I can almost understand why. Far better to cut her losses and run, than to face up to the fact that she'd left her other son with a cruel tyrant.'

'Oh, Loukas.'

She reached her hand towards his face as if to stroke his cheek but he caught her wrist in an iron-hard grip of his own. Turning her palm upwards, he ran his tongue slowly over the salty flesh, his eyes never leaving her face.

'I don't want your pity, Jess,' he said softly. 'That's not the reason I told you.'

She trembled beneath the lick of his tongue. 'Why *did* you tell me?'

He thought about it. It was more a question of why he had kept it hidden before but now he could see that he had been ashamed. Ashamed of the circumstances which had forged him. So hungry for his cool and classy Englishwoman that he had cultured a deliberate elusiveness, so that she would accept him for his present, and not his past.

But she had not accepted him at all. He had still not been good enough and maybe for someone like her, he never would be.

He didn't answer her question, but fixed her with a steady gaze. He remembered the way she'd breathlessly whispered that she loved him and how, for a short while, he had believed her. But words were easy, weren't they? His mother used to profess love, then leave him alone and frightened while she went out with her latest man. 'Why did you turn down my proposal?' he said suddenly.

She bit her lip and looked down at the rumpled sheets. 'Because...because I thought you were doing it to be chivalrous. To save me from my father's anger.'

'First time in my life I've ever been called chivalrous,' he said sardonically. 'But I don't think you're being entirely honest, are you, Jess? Maybe you did it to protect your fortune from a man who had nothing—who might want to marry you for all the wrong reasons?' he said, and the faint flush of colour to her cheeks told him everything he wanted to know.

'Well, there was that too,' she admitted haltingly, lifting her eyes to his as if she should be applauded for her honesty.

Loukas gave a bitter laugh. She had looked on him as someone with an eye for the main chance—able to provide her with sex, but best kept at arm's length when it came to permanency, or commitment.

And wasn't it crazy that *even now* it still hurt to realise that?

He didn't handle pain well. Physical pain was no problem, but emotional pain he found unendurable and he'd learnt that there was only one way to guarantee immunity. Don't get involved. Don't let anyone close enough to inflict it. It was a simple but effective rule as long as you stuck to it. And with Jess he'd been stupid enough to take his eye off the ball for a while.

'But you know something?' he questioned. 'You did me a kind of favour, in a way. I realised that marriage was completely wrong for someone like me.'

'Is that why you've never settled down with anyone else? Why you still live in luxury hotels, instead of having a real home?'

'Neh.' He gave a soft, cynical laugh. 'I've

grown used to my life. I wouldn't have it any other way.'

'And children? What about them?'

'What about them? Why the hell would I want to bring children in the world, just to screw them up? I know what that's like and so does my twin brother.'

'Right,' she said uncertainly.

He thought he could see a flicker of darkness in her eyes—as if his words were hurting *her*. As if she wanted to reach out and stroke his pain away. And he didn't need that. He didn't need her sympathy, or understanding. He didn't want her looking at him as if he were a puzzle she could solve, because he was fine just the way he was. He didn't want her making him *feel* stuff, because life was so much easier when you didn't. There were a million things he didn't want from her and only one thing he did.

He pulled her closer, so that he could feel the warm softness of her skin. Her face was turned up to his and her lips were eagerly parted, and for a while he just teased her. He brushed his mouth over hers—back and forth—until she made a sound halfway between frustration and desire. Sliding her hand around the back of his neck, she pulled him down towards her and he felt a heady rush of sexual power as she clung to him.

This, he thought, just before he kissed her— this was all he wanted from Jessica Cartwright.

CHAPTER EIGHT

WHAT A DIFFERENCE a day could make. Or a
night. A night when Loukas had seemed determined to show Jessica everything she'd been
missing.

Sex.

Her throat dried.

A devastating masterclass in desire and satisfaction.

She had hardly slept a wink and by rights
she should have felt terrible when she met the
crew to resume shooting the following morning. But terrible was the last thing she felt.
She felt *alive*. As if all her senses had suddenly exploded. The diamonds, which yesterday had hung like a millstone around her neck,
today made her feel pampered and decadent as
they glittered against her skin—and the close-
fitting silk of her bodice no longer felt con-
stricting. She was conscious of the way it clung

to her breasts—thrusting them upwards and giving her a bit of a cleavage and reminding her of the way Loukas had licked his way over every inch of them during the sensual night they'd shared.

'Wow,' said the photographer softly as she stood in the gondola—only today she had no trouble keeping her balance, despite the rocking motion of the distinctive craft. And when she was told to pout and look dreamy, she had no problem with that, either. In fact, it was difficult to look anything *but* dreamy when all she could think about was the man whose black eyes had grown opaque and smoky as he had lowered his head to kiss her.

But kisses could blind you to the reality and she had to keep reminding herself that it had only been about sex—*because how could it ever be anything else*? He'd made it clear that experience had hardened him. That he had changed and now there was no room in his life for marriage. She thought about the way his voice had grown cold when she'd asked about children, and—bearing in mind the things he'd told her—could she honestly blame him for not wanting any? All the things he'd told her about his childhood made her aware of just how grim his early life must have been. No wonder he'd been so reluctant to speak about it in the past. And then to discover out of the blue that he had a twin brother—a discovery like that must have rocked his world.

So she was going to have to be very mature. To accept the person he was, and if last night was the only night they would ever share, then she would accept that, too. No tears. No regrets. And definitely no recriminations. She'd had her chance a long time ago and she had blown it. She had no one to blame but herself.

This time Loukas didn't watch over the photo shoot, telling her he needed to work, before slipping away from her room in the early hours. She supposed he hadn't wanted anyone to see him leaving, knowing that it might muddy the waters if the crew discovered that the CEO was sleeping with the model.

She spent the entire day being photographed, but that ice-cube feeling was a distant memory. The ballgown was followed by a slinky white silk trouser suit, with nipped-in jacket and wide palazzo pants. The diamond necklace had been replaced with neat diamond studs and, with a nod to her previous career, she wore a tennis bracelet—a narrow

row of diamonds, which glittered discreetly at her wrist. The last shot of the day was of Jessica wearing a monochrome mini-dress, teamed with waterproof boots as she stood in the centre of a flooded St Mark's Square, and even though her arms were covered with goosebumps she didn't feel particularly cold. Patti fed her sips of hot coffee and torn-off little pieces of croissant. Tourists gathered to watch, only today she didn't mind, and when the art director called it a day and came over to congratulate her, she experienced a feeling of real achievement. She'd done what she had set out to do. She had pulled it out of the bag and given them what they wanted. She'd shown them—and herself—that she was capable of change, and wasn't that a very empowering feeling?

They all trooped back to the hotel through the echoing streets of the darkening afternoon and Loukas was just coming down the sweeping staircase, leaving Jessica wondering whether someone had rung ahead to tell him they were on their way. Her heart pounded as she watched him move, so dark and so vital, capturing the attention of every person in the place. He walked over to talk to the art director and she tugged the cashmere wrap closer, feeling her nipples tightening beneath the soft material, afraid someone might notice and work out why. They chatted intently for a moment and then he looked round, his black gaze sweeping around until it had found her, and her heart began to race even faster as he walked across the foyer towards her.

A faint smile lifted the edges of his mouth. 'I gather you excelled yourself today,' he said.

She smiled, trying to ignore the sudden yearning deep inside her. Trying to convince herself that she only felt this way because he was a powerful, alpha male she'd spent the night with and that was how nature had conditioned her to react. 'Thanks,' she said.

'I'm tempted to ask what has changed since yesterday,' he murmured. 'But I think we both know the answer to that, wouldn't you say, *koukla mou*?'

She tilted her chin. 'Are you looking for praise?'

'Why would I need to do that when you gave me all the praise I could possibly want last night?' His lashes shuttered down to half conceal the ebony glint of his eyes. 'Would you like to repeat some of it, in case you've forgotten?'

'That won't be necessary,' she said hastily. She could see Patti and the others moving towards the elevator—presumably to pack—and her heart grew heavy as she realised that it had all come to an end. *And she didn't want it to come to an end.* 'I guess I'd better go and pack as well.'

'Well, you could. Or you and I could stay on for an extra day and give ourselves a chance to see the city properly?'

She stared at him.

His eyes glittered. 'What's the matter, Jess—doesn't the idea appeal?'

'It's not that. Surely you have…' She tried to keep the tremor of excitement from her voice. She shrugged. 'Oh, I don't know. Work to do.'

'I'm the boss. Work can wait—while I, on the other hand…'

His words trailed off, smoky, suggestive and edged with a raw hunger which left her in no doubt what he was thinking. But it had been a long time since Jessica had engaged in sexual banter and she'd forgotten the first rule about keeping it light.

'What?' she whispered.

'I don't want to wait,' he said softly. 'And I don't intend to. I still want you. I want you so badly that I'm hard now, just standing this close to you. So hard that I want to rip those trousers from your delicious legs and put my hands where that silk has been.'

He had lowered his voice so that only she could hear, but even so Jessica found herself looking around, terrified that a passing guest would overhear, or that someone discerning would correctly interpret their body language.

'Loukas,' she said, only the word didn't come out as it was supposed to do. It came out all throatily, like a husky invitation instead of a protest.

He shook his head, as if pre-empting her objections. 'One night wasn't enough. Not nearly enough to cancel out eight long years of a slow-burning fever in my blood. A fever which has never quite gone away, no matter how many other women have graced my bed. Has it been like that for you too, Jess?' His voice dipped. 'I'm guessing so. Because you were wild for me last night. Wild,' he finished silkily.

Her instinct was to play it down. To clamp down on the feeling before it had started to grow and take hold. It was a survival mechanism which had served her well in the past. It meant she'd been able to accept a promising tennis career which had ended before it had even begun. It had enabled her to turn down his offer of marriage because she'd known that had been the right thing to do. And this time round she knew it would be best if they kept last night as a one-off. A single, amazing night they'd shared, which was never going to happen again. Because one night was easy to be objective about; any more than that and she was running straight into trouble.

She opened her mouth to say no, but something in his face was making the words die on her lips. Was it a sudden softness about the eyes which reminded her of the man he'd once been, before life had taken him and roughed him up even more?

Because something about the way he was looking at her touched a part of herself she'd thought had died a long time ago, and she was surprised he hadn't worked out for himself the reason why she'd been so *wild* for him last night. Not just because she'd been living in a sexual desert since he'd walked out of her life, but because he made her feel *stuff*. Stuff like joy and intense pleasure. Stuff like love.

She chewed on her lip. In the past she wouldn't have been able to spontaneously extend a trip abroad, because Hannah would have been at home and Jessica had always prided herself on being there for her. But Hannah was thousands of miles away and nobody else knew or cared where she was. She could think of that as isolation, or she could think of it as being free. A negative or a positive—the choice was hers.

'Okay,' she said. 'It seems a pity to come all this way and not see something of the city.'

He slanted her a conspiratorial smile. 'That's what I thought.'

Her hands were trembling as she went to her room to change into jeans, sweater and a waterproof jacket—almost glad that the day was grey and misty and she could put on normal clothes. The kind of clothes she wore at home, which made her feel more like herself and not some manufactured glamour puss.

She met Loukas back downstairs and they left the hotel, but soon after the narrow streets had begun to swallow them up, he steered her into a darkened bar.

'You need a drink,' he said firmly. 'And you missed out on lunch, didn't you?'

'It's nearly four o'clock, Loukas. We won't get lunch at this time.'

'I know that. But Venice is a city which is prepared for all eventualities.' He sat her gently down on a bar stool and nodded at the proprietor, who was polishing a glass. 'You drink a glass of local wine, which the locals call an *ombra*, and you eat some of these delicious little snacks, which are known as *cicchetti.* See? Tiny little plates of seafood, vegetables and polenta. Come on, Jess. Relax. Stop looking so uptight.' He lowered his voice. 'Pretend it's last night and I'm kissing you.'

Loukas wondered what she was thinking as she turned her remarkable eyes to his. He sensed a struggle within her, as if she was still fighting him off, and maybe it was that which drew him towards her. Was it her slight air of resistance—of *restraint*—which reinforced his growing realisation that this *thing* between them was still not settled?

Why not?

His jaw tightened. She should have been smitten with him by now—and that wasn't arrogance, it was fact. One night of sex was usually enough to guarantee adoration from whomever had shared his bed, and their history gave Jess more reason than most to have fallen under his spell. But that was the thing with her. The closer you got, the more she seemed to pull away, and all it did was to fire up his dominant hunter instincts. He sipped at his wine. Was that the reason he wanted her so much—because she kept him at arm's length unless he happened to be buried deep inside her body?

She sipped her wine, glancing round at the shadowy interior of the small bar as if soaking up the atmosphere.

'You seem to know your way around Venice pretty well,' she observed.

'I do. It was another part of my *grand tour*, even though I had nothing very much in my pockets when I first arrived.'

'So how did you survive?'

He shrugged. 'There is always work if you are prepared to do anything—and I was. I went to all the great European cities and set myself a goal. Six months in each, by which time I wanted to feel as comfortable as if I was a native of that city.'

'And was there any particular shortcut?'

'Not one that you'd probably want to hear.'

Her cheeks went pink. 'You mean—through women?'

He shrugged. 'I told you that you wouldn't like it.'

'It doesn't bother me at all.'

'Liar,' he said softly and leaned forward to brush his lips overs hers, tasting the wine and the warmth in that brief kiss. 'Want to see some more of Venice?'

She nodded and he found himself linking her fingers through his as they started walking along the canal. Her hands were cold and despite their tennis-honed strength they felt fragile and small within his. He found himself thinking that he didn't usually do this kind of thing. He didn't wander hand in hand with a woman, pointing out the secret churches and hidden squares and feeling high with the sheer beauty of the city, almost as if he'd never really seen it before.

The afternoon became devoid of all natural light and as the streetlights began to glow, the deserted streets took on the atmospheric feel so beloved of film-makers. Loukas saw someone snap on a light in one of the great flats along the Grand Canal and a golden glow spilled down, turning Jess's hair into molten gold. They wandered off down one of the narrow streets and he was thinking about taking her to that little bar near the Rialto, when he felt her tugging at his sleeve.

'Did you hear that?' she asked.

Frowning, he shook his head.

'Listen,' she said, putting her finger over her lips.

He frowned, but all he could hear was the lap of the water and the echoing sound of music coming from a long way off. 'I don't hear anything.'

'Shh! There it is again.'

And then he heard it—would have recognised it instantly if it hadn't held such poignant memories for him. The terrified sound of a child's cry. He stiffened, every sense on full alert as he began to move purposefully in the direction of the sound. He could hear Jess's rapid breathing beside him, just before he saw the huddled shape of a child ahead of them—a boy—his face streaked with tears, his brown eyes wide and frightened.

Jess began to run towards him, but Loukas caught her arm, speaking to her in English, in a low voice. 'Wait. Be careful,' he said.

'Be *careful*?' She turned on him. 'What are you talking about, Loukas? He's just a *child*.'

'And this could be a scam. It's a well-known method for fleecing tourists. Children used as decoys to lure unsuspecting foreigners. There are pickpockets in this city, just like everywhere else.'

Angrily, she shook his arm away. 'I don't care,' she said fiercely. 'I'm willing to take the risk of losing a few euros. I want to help him. Let me *go*!'

But he shadowed her as she ran forward and the boy turned his face upwards and choked out his frightened words.

'*Aiutami,*' he said. '*Aiuto.*'

Remorse flooded through Loukas as immediately he crouched and looked into the tear-filled eyes. 'I will help you,' he said gruffly, in the same language. 'Where are your parents?'

'I don't know!' cried the boy and Jess put her arms around him as if it was the easiest thing in the world, and Loukas felt his heart clench as he watched her soothing him, listening carefully to what the child said in a breathless dialect he thought might be Sicilian.

'He says he lost sight of his parents and when he heard them calling for him, he began to run,' he translated. 'Only he took the wrong turning and began to panic. He ran even faster, and that's when he realised he could no longer hear them. He couldn't hear anything. He isn't hurt, but he's frightened.'

'I'm not surprised,' she said fervently as she stroked the boy's curly hair. 'Venice is a beautiful city by day, but it must be scary if you're a child and you're lost. All that water.' She shivered. 'Tell him that we're going to help find his parents.'

Loukas nodded as he lifted the boy to his feet and began to speak in a calm, low voice before turning to her and meeting the question in her blue eyes.

'I've explained that we'll take him to the *questura*—the police,' he said. 'And that we'll probably find his parents there, waiting for him. Come on, Jess. He wants you to take his hand. Oh, and his name is Marco.'

'Marco,' she said softly as the little boy clung to her hip and wept.

CHAPTER NINE

'THAT POOR CHILD,' said Jessica as she switched on one of the lamps and the room was flooded with a soft golden light. 'He was absolutely terrified.'

'I'm not surprised,' said Loukas, shutting the door softly behind him. 'Getting lost in Venice age seven isn't something to be recommended.'

'Do you think he'll be okay?'

'He'll be fine.' He frowned. 'Are *you* okay?'

Jessica nodded, hoping her smile would convey a sense of serenity she was far from feeling. They were back in her hotel room where they'd discovered champagne sitting in an ice bucket, delivered by the grateful parents of Marco Pasolini. She and Loukas had bumped into the fraught and terrified couple outside the entrance to the police station, where they had taken the little boy, who had still been tightly holding her hand. A voluble reunion had followed, with Marco's mother alternately sobbing and scolding her young son, before scooping him into her arms and covering his face with endless kisses. His father, meanwhile—according to the translation which Loukas had provided afterwards—proceeded to offer them the use of his Sicilian villa, his ocean-going yacht or any other part of his extensive estates, any time they cared to use them.

But now that the worry and the drama had died away, Jessica was left feeling exhausted. The experience had shaken her up more than she'd realised and had only increased her growing sense of disassociation. She felt as if she shouldn't really be here, in this room, with Loukas. As if their passion of the night before had been something unplanned and probably regrettable and now, in the harsh light of day, she wasn't sure what they were supposed to do next. Would he start peeling off her clothes and expecting another acrobatic performance, like last night? She hoped not. She felt shy and inexperienced, as if she couldn't possibly live up to his expectations.

She thought about his instinctive reaction

when they'd stumbled across the lost child. He had thought it was a scam.

'I'm fine,' she said, taking off her jacket and realising that her legs felt a little shaky. She sat down on a chair very suddenly and looked at him. 'Why did you jump to the conclusion that Marco was a pickpocket? That was a pretty harsh and cynical thing to do, in the circumstances.'

He gave a short and bitter laugh. 'Because I spent too many years as a bodyguard, and suspicion is something which was drummed into me. Something I learnt to live with. If you work for one of the world's wealthiest men, threats come from the most unlikely directions—something I learnt to my own cost. You learn never to trust what you see, or to believe what you hear. That nothing is ever as it seems.'

'That seems a pretty grim way to live your life.'

He raised his eyebrows. 'A cup half empty, rather than half full?'

She nodded. 'Something like that.'

'Or you could say that way you stand less chance of disappointment. If you don't have raised expectations, then they can't be smashed,' he said, his ebony gaze locking with hers. 'You were brilliant with him, by the way,' he added slowly. 'A natural.'

She heard a note of surprise in his voice, which he couldn't quite disguise. 'Something you weren't expecting?'

He shrugged. 'I never had you down as the maternal type.'

Maybe, she thought, because he must find it hard to recognise the 'maternal type', if such a thing existed. His own mother had always put the men in her life first, so could she really blame him if his perception of others was warped—if he had no real experience on which to base his judgements? Or maybe because he remembered her as single-minded and focused, letting her tennis dominate her whole life.

'I don't know if I was born that way, but it's something I learnt,' she said slowly. 'I had to. I became something of a substitute mother for my half-sister.'

'The little girl who was always hiding your hairbrush?' He frowned. 'Hannah?'

Jessica smiled. Funny he should remember that. 'That's the one. When my dad...*our* dad...and her mum were killed, I stepped in to look after her. Well, I had to really.'

'No, you didn't,' he said suddenly, another frown darkening his face. 'Presumably you had a choice and you chose to look after her. How old was she?'

'Ten.'

'And you were, what—eighteen?'

She nodded, thinking how beautiful he looked, silhouetted against the Venetian skyline. The shutters were still open and the spotlighted dome of the magnificent Salute church, which stood behind the wide band of gleaming water, could be seen in all its splendour.

'Yes,' she said. 'I was eighteen. The authorities wanted to foster her out to a proper family, but I fought very hard to keep her. I didn't...' Her words tailed off.

'Didn't what?'

She hesitated. She kept things locked inside her because that was what she'd been trained to do, just as she'd been trained to use a double-handed backhand. And when you did something for long enough it became a habit. A bit like Loukas, when he saw only danger around him. If you built a wall around your emotions you were safer—at least, that was the theory. But the rush of emotions she'd experienced today, following the incredible sex of last night, had left her feeling…

She wasn't sure. She didn't feel like Jessica Cartwright, that was for sure.

'I didn't want to let her go. Not because I loved her.' She cleared her throat. 'But probably because I didn't—at least, not at first. We'd never had an easy relationship. She was the adored child of two people who were very much in love, while I was the cuckoo in the nest—the offspring of the first marriage, a bad marriage, a marriage which should never have happened. At least, that's what I once heard my dad telling my stepmum. Hannah was always on the inside, in the warmth, while I always seemed to be out in the cold, literally, on the practice courts. And I think Hannah was a bit jealous of my tennis career. She used to hide my hairbrush, and sometimes my tennis racquet. She even threw away this stupid little mascot I carried around, until my father told me that champions didn't need mascots—they needed technique and determination.'

'So why did you fight so hard to keep her?'

'Because she was on her own and hurting,' she said simply. 'How could I not reach out to her?' But it hadn't been easy, because Jessica had been lost and hurting, too. She had missed her father. She had missed her career. And she'd missed Loukas. She'd missed him more than she could ever have imagined.

She realised she was cold. She was hugging her arms tightly around herself and wishing she hadn't taken off her jacket, especially now that Loukas's hard black gaze was sweeping over her.

'Why don't you go and take a bath?' he suggested roughly.

Awkwardly, she got to her feet. 'Good idea,' she said and went off into the bathroom, suddenly feeling self-conscious and realising that he hadn't touched her since they'd got back. Maybe he felt as cautious as she did, she thought as she upended lime and orange oil into the water and slowly lowered her aching body into the tub. Perhaps he'd realised that there was too much history for them to be able to enjoy a casual affair. Or maybe she wasn't capable of operating on that level.

Because already her feelings for him were changing. Minute by minute, she could feel it happening. She'd started to care what he thought of her. She'd started searching for emotions in his dark eyes. And it was a waste of time. He'd been completely honest about his reasons for wanting to have sex with her again—so why try to make it into something it wasn't? Embarking on a quest to make it into something it could never be was only ever going to bring her heartbreak.

She lay in the water for a long time—long enough for the skin at the ends of her fingers to become white and wrinkled. Long enough for Loukas to have grown bored with waiting, and to have made his escape, perhaps leaving behind a note scribbled on a piece of hotel notepaper. Because he certainly wasn't knocking at the bathroom door, asking her how long she was going to be.

Was he aware that a strange kind of shyness had crept over her as they'd stared at one another over the head of little Marco? That in that moment, she had glimpsed the little boy he'd once been and all the sadness he had known. She'd found herself thinking of the children she might have had with him. But Loukas doesn't want children, she reminded herself. He had been very clear about that.

Dragging a brush through her damp hair, she put on the massive bathrobe which was hanging on the back of the door and padded barefoot into her room, to find Loukas stretched out in one of the chairs, seemingly fast asleep. His eyes were closed and his face looked curiously relaxed as classical music drifted out from an unseen sound system.

She stood there, uncertain of whether or not she should wake him, when his lashes flickered apart and she was caught in the gleam of his ebony eyes.

'Hi,' he said softly. 'Good bath?'

She nodded, the lump in her throat making it impossible for her to speak because as he'd asked the innocent question it had sounded so heartbreakingly...*domestic*. It mocked her and taunted her with its implied intimacy. A real intimacy, which they'd never really shared.

There was a sudden knock on the door and she looked at him.

'Room Service,' he said, in answer to the question in her eyes

'I didn't order anything from Room Service.'

'No, but I did. Why don't you just get into bed, Jess? You look shattered. And don't look at me as if I'm the big, bad wolf, *koukla mou*.' His voice dipped. 'I am perfectly capable of being in the same room without leaping on you.'

She nodded, feeling the see-sawing of her own emotions in response to the things he was saying. She hadn't wanted sex, but suddenly she was finding that maybe she did. Only he seemed more concerned with getting his dinner!

But at least his back was turned as he answered the door, so that he wouldn't see her nakedness as she let the bathrobe slide to the floor before getting quickly into bed. It felt blissful as she sank into the mattress, the sheet cool and smooth beneath her clean skin, the duvet falling on top of her like a big, soft cloud.

She told herself she wasn't hungry but she must have been, because when he brought the food over to her—some sort of vegetable broth, followed by a toasted cheese sandwich—she began to devour it with an appetite which felt heightened. Comfort food, that was what they called food like this, and never had a description seemed more apt. After she'd finished she lay back against the feathery bank of pillows as the sound of violins filtered softly through the air.

'Better?' he questioned.

'Much.' She yawned. 'I didn't know you liked classical music.'

'Too brutish a sound for a rough, tough ex-bodyguard?' His eyes glittered. 'You thought I'd be more into heavy metal?'

Too comfortable to object, Jessica smiled lazily. 'Something like that.'

'Why don't you close your eyes, Jess? Stop fighting it. You look exhausted.'

His deep accent was lulling her. It felt like velvet pressing against her skin. She wanted to ask him what he was planning, but her eyelids were heavy and she thought about his words and wondered what she was trying to fight. She drifted into a sleep which was light enough to feel the mattress dip when he got in beside her. He pulled her against him and the pleasant shock of honed muscle and warm skin told her that he, too, was naked. Did that mean he *did* want sex?

'Loukas,' she mumbled.

'Shh,' he said, his arms tightening around her waist as he pulled her even closer and the room fell into darkness as he clicked off the lamp.

She must have slept because when she drifted back into consciousness, it was to find her head pillowed comfortably against his shoulder, her lips right next to the burr of his unshaven jaw. She kissed it. She couldn't help it; her lips seemed programmed to brush over that proud curve. He mumbled something as his hand slid down to cup her bottom while the other reached behind her head and guided her lips towards his.

That first kiss was lazy. It seemed to happen in slow motion, as if they had all the time in the world. As if she'd never really kissed him properly before. And maybe she hadn't. Beneath the protective cloak of darkness it seemed that there were a million ways to explore a man's mouth, and Jessica was about to discover every one of them. She could feel him smile as, slowly, she traced the tip of her tongue over the cushioned surface. He gave a murmur of satisfaction as she pressed kiss after little kiss against him. His body felt warm and comfortable against hers and soon she began to trickle her fingertip over his chest, allowing it to continue its path inexorably downwards. But he stopped her when she reached the dark whorls of hair which lay at the base of his belly, wreathing the sudden hard jerk of his erection.

'No. Not yet,' he said urgently. 'I'm so turned on, I hardly dare risk putting on a condom.'

She swallowed, because something about his words had sent crazy thoughts splintering into her mind. 'But you will?'

'Yes, I will. Even though I long to feel myself naked inside you. My skin bare against your skin. My seed in your body.'

His words excited her, but presumably that had been his intention. They reminded her that for Loukas this was all about technique—a bit like tennis, really. It might feel deep and emotional and highly intimate, but that was her stuff. Her stupid desires. And she mustn't give into them. She mustn't.

But it was hard not to be swept away when he was kissing each of her breasts with a thoroughness which felt almost like tenderness. Or when he lifted her up effortlessly to slide her down on top of him, murmuring silky words in Greek which sounded almost *loving*. Suspecting that he would want to watch her moving up and down on him, she waited for him to reach over and put the light on—but he didn't. And the lack of a spotlight on her face meant that she could give into what she really wanted to do, and what she wanted to do more than anything was not hold back. So she tangled her fingers in this thick hair and she told him he was beautiful. And if his big body stiffened for a moment and she sensed his sudden suspicion, that was quickly forgotten when she rode him with a determination which suddenly seemed outside her own control.

'Jess,' he gasped, and she'd never heard him say her name like that before.

But then her thoughts were blotted out and her body tensed around him.

And the most stupid thing of all was that she found herself wishing that he *hadn't* worn a condom.

CHAPTER TEN

'THESE ARE AMAZING,' said Gabe Steel slowly. 'Probably the most amazing transformation I've seen all year. Cinderella doesn't come close to it.'

Loukas stared at the mocked-up advert which covered most of the advertising chief's large desk and drank in the images staring back at him. Jessica Cartwright looking like he'd never imagined she could look. Who would have thought it? He shook his head slightly. He'd stayed away on the second day of the shoot and knew the crew had been pleased with the results, but even so. Hard to believe this was the same Jess who wore classy clothes in shades of cream and taupe while her sensible ponytail bobbed behind her. The same Jess who had stood wobbling awkwardly in the gondola during the first shoot, looking like a little girl dressed up in her mother's clothes.

His throat tightened.

The black and white photos were broken only by the magenta gleam of her lips and the Lulu ribbon which lay in a gleaming swirl by her feet. Against the imposing backdrop of the iconic city, she tipped her head at an angle and looked straight into the lens. Her breasts were highlighted by the low-cut bodice, showcasing the diamonds which blazed like ice fire next to her pale skin. A gentle breeze had lifted the blonde hair so that the blunt-cut strands whipped around her chin, and her smoky eyes were emphasised by the heavy fringe.

But it was more than her beauty or the air of fragility she seemed to project, or even the way her eyes seemed full of a strange, clear light. She personified sex…that was the thing. It radiated from every pore of her body. It was there in every gesture she made. The pout of her lips was defiant and the hand slung carelessly against her jutting hip made her look like every man's fantasy come true. The teenage sweetheart was all grown up.

'What the hell happened to her?' Gabe was asking, his eyes narrowing as he looked at Loukas.

Loukas didn't answer. How could he possibly answer, when he knew it would sound like some kind of chest-thumping macho boast if he told the truth? *She looks like a woman who has just been thoroughly ravished and I should know because I was the one doing the ravishing.*

And that was another shock to the system. He hadn't expected the sex to be so good. He'd thought that once the novelty of having her in his arms again had worn off, he would realise that there were plenty of lovers more exciting than Jessica Cartwright. He'd tried to convince himself that he had built up the memory of their lovemaking in his mind to be something it wasn't. Only it hadn't turned out that way. It had been mind-blowing. Every time. He'd felt as if he were touching the stars. He'd spent his entire time in the city in a dazed and permanent state of arousal.

Was that why he had persuaded her to stay on? Why one night had turned into two and then three? He'd intended them to fly back to England the day after they'd returned Marco to his parents, but something had stopped him and he told himself it must have been sex. But there had been something else which had made him want to prolong it, and that had been the nagging certainty that this relationship would not survive the cold light of reality. A love affair in Venice was one thing, when you could get swept away by the history and the atmosphere and the sheer beauty of the city. But life back in the UK, with their normal lives threatening to collide? No way.

He realised that Gabe was still staring at him, waiting for a reply to his question.

'I guess she grew up,' said Loukas simply.

'You know we have to capitalise on this?' said Gabe. 'Give the campaign a kick-start. Show the world that this is going to be big...'

Almost absently Loukas nodded as he studied the shot of her in the black and white dress and a pair of rubber boots, standing ankle-deep in water in a flooded St Mark's Square. They'd caught her looking up at something overhead—a bird?—and she was *giggling* and, despite being all grown up, suddenly she looked about eighteen again. Something clenched at his heart. 'How?' he questioned huskily.

'We throw a cocktail party for the press at the Granchester on Monday night, with the new look Jessica as the guest of honour.'

Loukas frowned. 'Isn't that a little short notice?'

'Not on a Monday—and not with your name attached to the invitation,' said Gabe drily. 'It's amazing the space people can find in their diaries if the person holding the party is influential enough. I'll get Patti to sort out Jessica's wardrobe and make sure she has something suitable to wear.' He frowned. 'Another dress, I think, and some of the best gems in your collection. But not diamonds this time. Let's go for something different.'

'Sapphires,' said Loukas slowly, and the thought of the darker hue contrasting with the aquamarine gleam of her eyes sent a thrill of desire skittering over his skin. 'She will wear my sapphires.'

Jessica stared at herself in the mirror. This time the dress was blue, and her jewellery gleamed as darkly as the midnight sky. She lifted her hand to her hair, watching her reflection mimicking the movement, her fingertips brushing against a small sapphire and diamond clip which glittered like starlight.

The sound of a footfall disturbed her and as she looked up to see Loukas reflected back in the glass, her heart began to pound erratically.

'You look beautiful,' he said.

She closed her eyes and shivered as he lowered his head to plant a kiss on one bare shoulder. 'Do I?'

'You know you do. You don't need me to tell you that, Jess.'

But that was where he was wrong—she *did*. She stared at his dark, bent head. She still felt like someone playing dress-up. She still felt vulnerable—especially since they'd arrived back in England and Loukas had persuaded her to stay in London. He'd told her that it was crazy not to use her luxury suite at the Vinoly Hotel, while they continued to *enjoy* one another. He had said this while trickling one finger over the swell of her naked breast and she hadn't really been in a position to say no. In fact she hadn't been in a position to do anything except make love, which was what he had been doing to her at the time.

But the reality of being in London like this didn't sit comfortably. Loukas went into the office each morning, and although she made sure that she took advantage of all that the city had to offer—including a gorgeous exhibition of Victorian embroidery—she felt like a fish out of water. As if she was waiting all the time. Waiting for him.

And Loukas seemed…well…*different*. She stifled a sigh. It wasn't something she could put her finger on. Was his lovemaking more cold-blooded than it had been in Venice, or was that just her imagination? It wasn't something she could really discuss with him without causing offence—and she didn't want to offend him. She wanted… She stared at his reflection in the mirror as he continued to kiss his way along her shoulder… She didn't know what she wanted, only that it was unlikely to involve roses and moonlight. Not from him. She sensed that for him it was already over, like when you turned an egg timer and the sand started to trickle away—the countdown had begun.

But she wasn't going to let him see her insecurities or her fears. She was going to take it all in her stride, because she was good at doing that. So as he lifted his lips from her shoulder she was able to smile so widely that she almost convinced herself she was happy. She thought about the evening ahead and sent him a slightly anxious look. 'So all I have to do tonight is chat to people and twirl around?'

'You've got it in one. Why don't you practise now?' His voice lowered. 'Twirl around. Go on.'

'Loukas.' Something in his face was turning her stomach to jelly. 'You…mustn't.'

'Mustn't what?'

Her voice sounded breathless. 'You can't kiss me now because my lipstick will—'

'Tough,' he said darkly, blotting out all her objections and kissing her so thoroughly that afterwards she had to apply the magenta-coloured gloss all over again.

But his behaviour during the short journey to the Granchester seemed to reinforce her growing insecurity. Nobody would have ever guessed they were a couple because he made no outward sign that they were anything more than working colleagues. He didn't touch her, or take her hand in his. There was no complicit smile which might indicate to the world that she was sharing his bed. Tonight she was very definitely the employee and he the boss, and she found herself thinking that their relationship had always been defined by secrecy.

A barrage of photographers was waiting outside the hotel and she kept her smile pinned to her lips as she was dazzled by the blinding wall of flash which greeted their arrival. Because she knew they weren't just here to see the jewellery. They were here to gaze in curiosity at her new, glossy image. They were hoping that she had bitten off more than she could chew, because there was nothing the press liked more than to bear witness to failure...

Inside, the Venetian photos had been blown up and mounted on the walls, so that they dominated the smaller of the Granchester's two ballrooms. Everywhere she looked she could see herself and, once Jessica had become acclimatised to the slightly surreal sensation, she found herself glancing round in disbelief. She looked so *different*. But it wasn't just the sharp new haircut or the heavier than usual make-up. It wasn't even the dress or the diamonds which made her look so unrecognisable. It was the shining look in her eyes—as if she were nursing the most beautiful secret in the world.

And Jessica realised with a jolt that she looked like a woman...if not actually *in* love, then certainly bordering on the edges of it.

But the camera lied. She knew that.

Pushing aside her confused thoughts, she tried to work the room as she knew she should. She spoke to a couple of women who worked on glossy magazines and was introduced to a man who wrote the diary section of an up-market tabloid. But despite her outward air of confidence, she found it impossible to relax, especially as Loukas was on the other side of the room and had barely acknowledged her all evening.

She didn't dare eat anything for fear of smudging her lips and the single sip of cock-tail she indulged in felt strong enough to blow her head off. This isn't my world, she thought desperately. It never really was. Everyone else seemed to know their own place in it, but not her. The smile plastered to her lips felt forced and she was terrified her conversation sounded dull to these urban high-flyers. Because they sure as hell weren't interested in talking about embroidery or growing vegetables.

It was with a feeling of relief that she saw Patti and slipped into a corner to talk to the stylist, feeling relaxed for the first time all evening, when suddenly she glanced across the room to see Loukas deep in conversation with a brunette. He'd been talking to other women, of course—she'd clocked that—but this seemed more...*intimate*.

The woman was wearing a sparkly dress so

short that it made Jessica's own feel as if it had been borrowed from a museum. He was leaning his head forward to listen intently and as the woman spoke her dark hair swayed like a glossy mahogany curtain. Jessica could feel herself tensing as she saw him laugh and Patti must have noticed the direction of her glance, because she turned her head and smiled.

'Yeah. Stunning, isn't she? *And* she's French. Used to be a human rights lawyer before she started writing for one of the papers and now she's one of the best-paid feature writers in the country. Life is so unfair, isn't it?'

Don't ask it, Jessica urged herself. *Just don't ask it.*

She asked it.

'They seem to know each other very well?'

Patti smiled. 'Yeah. I think they were lovers for a while, in Paris.'

'Really?' Jessica wondered if that squeaking reply was really her voice. Was that sick pounding of her heart due to an unwanted wave of *jealousy* which she had no right to feel?

She tried not to let it spoil the rest of the evening, telling herself she wasn't even going to mention it. Even in the car on the way back to the hotel, she managed to make small talk and to look suitably pleased when Loukas told her how happy everyone was with her performance.

He brushed his hand over her waist as they stopped outside her suite and reached into her bag for her key card.

'Hey,' he said softly. 'Want to come to mine?'

'Not tonight. Would you mind?' She forced a smile. 'I'm very tired.'

'So?' He stroked a reflective fingertip over her ribcage. 'Haven't I proved that I'm capable of letting you sleep, even if having you naked beside me drives me crazy with desire?'

'Who was that woman?'

Her blurted question seemed to come out of nowhere and he raised his eyebrows. 'There were a lot of women there this evening, Jess.'

'The brunette. The one in the mini-dress.'

'Ah, yes. Maya.' He smiled. 'Her name is Maya.'

Heart pounding, she pushed open the door and walked inside and he followed her.

'Why, were you jealous?' he continued, almost conversationally.

'No.'

'Liar.' He gave a soft laugh. 'You were. You are. I can read it on your face.'

And that was Jessica's wake-up call. He wasn't *supposed* to be reading *anything* on her face, because one of her great strengths was to hide her feelings behind a cool mask. *Wasn't* it? If he'd started seeing things like jealousy in her eyes, how soon before he started seeing other things, too? Stuff she was trying to deny even to herself because she knew that it was pointless. Stuff like still caring for him when she knew there was no future in it. Stuff like falling in love with him all over again.

And then a thought occurred to her and a terrible wave of suspicion washed over her, so that she had to fight it like crazy. She knew he was ruthless. He'd told her he was ruthless. Had he...had he deliberately gone out of his way to make her fall for him, just so that he could do to her what she'd done to him all those years ago?

'Like I said, I'm very tired.'

His face darkened. 'Is Maya the reason for the icy look and frozen behaviour? Is talking to an ex-lover such a terrible thing to do when I meet her socially? What would you have me do, Jess? Tell her I'm sorry, but I happen to be sleeping with someone who wants to keep me on a leash?'

She shook her head, telling herself that she was being stupid but it didn't seem to help. *Because this was the world he operated in. A world full of sophisticated ex-lovers he bumped into at parties and then made as if it didn't matter. Because it didn't.* Not to him. A man didn't get a reputation as a playboy because he sat at home every night, nursing a cup of cocoa. Playboys had partners. Lots of them. Playboys were known mainly for the fact that they never settled down, and she needed to accept that. You didn't get a second chance in life. Not with someone like Loukas.

'Of course not,' she said. 'It was completely unreasonable and I don't know what came over me.'

He tilted her chin with his fingers so that she had nowhere to look except into the dark gleam of his eyes. 'So what shall we do to make it better?'

It wasn't easy but she gave the smile she knew was expected of her. The one with just the right amount of flirtation. One which managed to convey that she'd just had a temporary blip, but that everything was fine again.

Except that it wasn't. She felt as if she were standing on the edge of a cliff which had started to crumble and any minute now she would lose her footing and fall, if she wasn't sensible enough to take a step back.

This wasn't going anywhere. She'd known that from the beginning. So get out now, before it's too late.

Putting her arms around his neck, she drew him close and heard his soft laugh as he slid down the zip of her dress with practised fingers. She closed her eyes as his fingers found her bare skin and, automatically, she began to shiver.

Once more, she told herself.

One more night.

CHAPTER ELEVEN

SHE WAS GONE when he returned from work next evening and as Loukas looked at the single sheet of paper which was all that was left of her, he realised that it came as no great surprise. Last night in his arms, she had been mind-blowing but he'd sensed something in the way she'd kissed him before he'd left for work that morning…a certain sadness which no amount of sexual chemistry could disguise. Her lips had lingered on his in a way which had seemed wistful rather than provocative. And when he stopped to think about it, hadn't there been a little catch in her voice as she'd said goodbye?

He hadn't needed to read the few words she'd written on hotel notepaper to know that she wasn't planning on coming back.

He stared at it.

Thanks.

He frowned. For *what*, exactly? The job or the sex?

I had a fabulous time in Venice, and I'm glad that the photos were such a success, but I'm missing Cornwall and I have a garden which is missing me.
Take good care of yourself, Loukas.
Jess.

She hadn't even put a kiss, she'd just drawn one of those stupid, smiley faces and he screwed up the sheet of paper, crushing it viciously in the palm of his hand. She'd walked out on him. She'd turned her back on him. Again. She was arrogant, she was haughty and he didn't need this.

He did not need this.

Stalking over to the drinks cabinet, he poured himself a glass of vodka and tossed it back in one deft mouthful, the way Dimitri had taught him.

Only the liquor didn't do what it was supposed to do. It didn't douse the fury which had started to flame inside him. It didn't stop

him from wanting to haul her into his arms
and…what?

Have sex with her?

Yes. His mouth twisted. That was what he
wanted.

All he wanted.

He paced around his suite, wondering why
tonight it felt like a cage, despite the unparal-
leled luxury of the fixtures and fittings. Because he'd grown used to having her just along
the corridor—was that it? And how the hell
could that happen in such a short time?

Because it hadn't *been* a short time, he realised. This had been bubbling away under the
surface for years.

He forced himself to concentrate on work,
losing himself in the negotiations to open a
branch of Lulu in Singapore's Orchard Road.
And there was other good news which should
have helped put Jessica Cartwright into the
background of his mind. His sales team in-
formed him excitedly that sales of precious
stones in the London store alone had shot up
by a staggering twenty-five per cent following the Valentine's Day advert—and they were
planning to use the same advertisement on a
global basis. It really *was* going to be big.

He went to the gym every night for punishing workouts, which left his body exhausted but his mind still racing. He turned down dinner invitations and threw himself into his work, which for once did not provide its all-encompassing distractions.

But life went on and the press was still going crazy. Gabe Steel phoned to say that his agency had been fielding calls from media outlets ever since Jess's piece had gone to press, since everyone was keen to discover how the sporty tennis star had transformed herself into such a vamp. Would she like to give an interview to one of the papers? Would she do a short slot on breakfast TV, or the even more popular mid-morning show? Were they planning to use her in another campaign any time soon?

'And?' bit out Loukas. 'It was supposed to be a one-off.'

'I know, but we'd be crazy not to capitalise on this,' said Gabe. 'The trouble is that nobody can get hold of her. She isn't answering her phone, or her emails. I'm thinking of sending—'

'No. Don't bother doing that. I'll go,' said Loukas, and it wasn't until he'd put the phone down that it occurred to him that Gabe hadn't questioned why the company boss should be chasing down to the other end of the country after some random model.

He set off early in the morning, just as the sun was beginning to rise and the roads were empty, save for the occasional lorry. It was a long time since he'd been to Cornwall and it brought back memories of a different life. He remembered the first time he'd seen it. His Russian boss had owned huge chunks of land there, as well as mooring one of his boats in Padstow—and the summer he'd spent there had been the most glorious of his life. For a boy brought up in the crowded backstreets of Athens, it had felt like a different world to Loukas. The wildness and the beauty. The sense of being remote. The salty air and the crash of the ocean. As the roads began to narrow into lanes and he passed through picture-perfect little villages, he thought how little had really changed.

And wasn't it funny how your feet automatically guided you to a place you hadn't seen in eight long years? The Cartwright mansion could still be seen from a distance, like some shining citadel outlined against the crisp blue of the winter sky, with its mullioned windows and its soaring roofs, and the lavender-edged gardens which swept right down to the cliffs. Across to one side, where the land was flatter, was the footpath which passed the tennis court where once he had watched Jess practise.

But when he rang the doorbell, a woman in her thirties appeared—a small child hiding behind her legs. The woman smiled at him and automatically touched her hair.

'Can I help you?'

He frowned, trying to work out who she could possibly be. 'I'm looking for Jess. Jessica.'

'Cartwright?'

'That's right.'

'She doesn't live here any more. We bought it from the people she sold it to. She's up on Atlantic Terrace now—near the cliff path. The little house right on the end, the one with the crooked chimney—do you know it?'

He didn't know it but he nodded, his mind working overtime as he thanked the woman and parked his car in the village, telling himself it was because he needed the exercise and not because he didn't want to be seen by Jess as he approached.

But that wasn't strictly true. His thoughts

were reeling and he was trying to make some sense of them. Had she sold up to simplify her life, or because it was too big for her and her half-sister?

He found what was in fact a cottage and it was small. Very small. He rapped loudly on the door, but there was no reply and suddenly he wondered what he was going to do if she'd gone away. She could be anywhere. He didn't know a single thing about her daily life, he realised. He'd imagined her life staying exactly the same, while his own had moved on. It had been part of his fixed image of Jess—the upper-class blonde in her country mansion. Because wasn't it easier to be angry with a stereotype than with a real person?

He walked to the back of the property and that was where he found her, attacking the bare earth furiously with a spade. She didn't hear him at first and as he found himself looking at the denim tightening over her buttocks, it was difficult not to appreciate the sheer grace of her movements.

She must have heard him, or sensed him, because suddenly she whirled round—her face growing through a whole series of emotions but so rapidly that he couldn't make out a single one except for the one which settled there, and it was one which was distinctly unwelcoming.

She leant heavily on the spade as if she needed it for support. 'What are you doing here, Loukas?'

'Parakalo,' he said sardonically. 'Nice to see you, too.'

She seemed to remember herself and forced a cool smile.

'Sorry. It just came as a bit of a shock, you creeping up on me like that.'

'Creeping?' he echoed.

'You know what I mean.' She shrugged, but the movement seemed to take a lot of effort. 'I mean, obviously, you're not just passing.'

'Obviously.'

She looked at him with her eyebrows raised as if she wanted him to help her out, but something stubborn had taken residence inside him and he didn't feel like helping her out.

'So why are you here?'

It was a question he'd been asking himself during the four-and-a-half-hour drive but had given up on it because he couldn't seem to find a satisfactory answer. 'You haven't been answering your phone. Or your emails.'

She held her finger to her lips and began to tap them, as if considering his accusation. 'I don't think that's written into my contract.'

'Maybe it isn't,' he said, feeling a nerve beginning to flicker at his temple. 'But I don't think it's unreasonable of us to want to get hold of you, is it?'

'*Us?*'

'Zeitgeist,' he bit out, wondering what the hell was the matter with her. Why she was being so damned stubborn. And so remote. Hadn't they just spent the best part of a week being about as intimate as a man and woman could be? 'And Lulu,' he added. 'You know. The people who provided you with work.'

'I was told it was a one-off.' She gripped the handle of the spade. 'And you were the one who told me that.'

'With hindsight, I might have spoken a little hastily.'

Her gaze was steady. 'If only we all had the benefit of hindsight, Loukas.'

He frowned. He didn't want this impenetrable *wall* between them. He wanted her onside. 'The campaign has been a huge success.'

'Ah.' She smiled. 'The campaign.'

'We've been inundated with requests for interviews, TV—'

'So have I,' she said sharply. 'My answer machine keeps getting filled up with messages, even though I clear it at the end of every day.'

'But you didn't think to answer them?'

'Actually, I did. And then decided not to.' She wrapped her jacket more tightly around herself and gave an exaggerated shiver. 'I'm getting cold just standing here.'

'Then why don't you take me inside and offer me some of your legendary English hospitality?'

Jessica hesitated when she heard the sarcasm in his voice, but she could hardly say no. And the trouble was that she didn't want to say no. She wanted to know what had brought him here—appearing on her horizon like some dark avenging angel. Most of all she wanted him to kiss her, and that was where the danger lay. She had missed him so much that it had hurt and yet now that she had seen him again her heart had started aching even more. This was a lose-lose situation and his presence here wasn't going to help her in the long term.

But you couldn't really turn a man away when he'd driven all this way to see you, could you?

'You'd better come in,' she said.

He followed her into the kitchen and she could sense him looking around as she put the kettle on. What did he think of her dresser, with the eclectic collection of jugs, or the cork board studded with all the postcards which Hannah had sent from her travels? Was he comparing it to his huge but cold suite at the Vinoly and did it all look terribly *parochial* to his sophisticated eye?

The wind had ruffled his black hair and he was dressed in jeans more faded than hers, along with a battered brown leather jacket. His casual clothes started playing tricks with her memory. Like a flashback, they gave her a glimpse of the man he had once been. The big bear of a bodyguard who used to watch her from the side of a tennis court. But flashbacks were notoriously unreliable—they always painted the past in such flattering shades that you wanted to be back there. And that was impossible. The past was the refuge for losers who couldn't cope with the present, and she wasn't going to be one of those losers.

She made tea and took the tray into the small sitting room which overlooked the Atlantic. She thought about lighting a fire but then decided against it, because he wasn't staying long. He definitely wasn't staying long.

'So...' She put a steaming star-decorated mug on a small table beside one of the chairs, but he didn't take the hint to sit down—he just strode over to the window and stood there, staring out at the crashing ocean, his silhouetted body dark and powerful and more than a little intimidating.

He turned back, eyes narrowed. 'Did you move because the house was too big?'

She thought about saying yes. It would be understandable, after all—especially now that it was just her. But Jessica knew that she couldn't keep hiding behind her cool mask, thinking that to do so would offer her some kind of protection. Because she'd realised that it didn't. Masks didn't stop you wishing for things which were never going to come true. And they didn't stop your heart from hurting when you fell for men who were wrong for you.

'No,' she said. 'I moved because I had to. Because my father had built up massive debts which were only revealed after he was killed in the avalanche.'

His eyes narrowed, but there wasn't a flicker of emotion on his own face. And suddenly she was glad that he hadn't come out with the usual platitudes which people always trotted out, platitudes which meant zero and somehow ended up making you feel even worse. Maybe they were more alike than she'd thought. Or maybe now that they had entered the dark worlds of death and debts, he suddenly felt on familiar ground.

He sat down then, lowering his mighty frame into a chair which up until that moment had always looked substantial.

'What happened?'

She watched as he picked up his tea and sipped it. 'Like everyone else, he was banking on me winning a Grand Slam, or three. He was very ambitious.' She shrugged. 'They say that fathers make the best and the worst coaches.'

'You didn't like him very much,' he said slowly.

His words came out of the blue. Few people would have thought it and even fewer would have dared say it. It would be easier to deny it but her chin stayed high and defiant as she met his eyes with a challenge. 'Does that shock you?'

He gave a hard smile in response. 'Very little in life shocks me, *koukla mou*.'

The soft Greek words slid over her skin, touching her at a time when she was feeling vulnerable, but she tried not to be swayed by them. She cleared her throat. 'He did his best. He did what he thought was right. It's just that he never really allowed me to have a normal life.'

'So why didn't you stand up to him?'

Recognising that his question was about more than the unbending routine of her tennis years, Jessica picked up a match and struck it to the crumpled-up paper in the grate, seeing the heated flare as it caught the logs and hoping it would warm the sudden chill of her skin. Because sometimes it was easier to be told what to do than to think for yourself. It meant you could blame someone else if it all went wrong. And it was hard to admit that, even to herself.

'There were lots of reasons why I didn't stand up to him, but I suppose what you really want to know is why I wasn't stronger when it came to you. Why I let him drive a wedge between us.' She sensed that he was holding his breath but she couldn't look at him. She didn't dare. Because if she removed her mask completely—mightn't he be repulsed by the face he saw beneath?

She threw an unnecessary log onto the fire. 'I thought we were too young to settle down and my career was very important to me.'

'But that's not the only reason, is it, Jess?'

There was a pause. 'No.' Her voice sounded quiet against the crackle of the fire. She stared into the forest of flames, losing herself in that flickering orange kingdom. 'I was an unsettled child. My parents split up when I was very young. My dad left my mum for a younger woman who was already pregnant with his child—Hannah—and my mum never really got over that. I lived with her shame and her bitterness, which didn't leave much room for anything else.'

She picked up her tea and cupped her hands around it. 'When she died I went to live with my father and that's when the tennis really kicked off. At last I had something to believe in. Something I could lose myself in. But my stepmother resented the amount of time it took him away from her and I think Hannah was a bit jealous of all the attention I got.' She gave a slightly nervous laugh. 'I mean, I'm probably making it sound worse than it was, but it was—'

'It sounds awful,' he interjected and she found herself having to blink back the sudden threat of tears, because his sympathy was unexpectedly potent.

'I'd already learnt not to show my feelings,' she said. 'And that became a useful tactic on the tennis court. Soon I didn't know how to be any other way. I learnt to block my emotions. Not to let anything or anyone in. Now do you understand?'

He nodded. 'I think so.'

'I didn't want to make you any promises I couldn't keep,' she rushed on. 'And marriage was an institution I didn't trust.'

But it had been more than that. On an instinctive level she had recognised that Loukas was a man who had been in short supply of love, who needed to be loved properly. And hadn't she thought herself incapable of that?

'There's something else,' he said. 'Something you're not telling me.'

It hurt that he could be so perceptive. She didn't want him to be perceptive—she wanted him to be brash and uncaring. She wanted him to reinforce that she'd done the right thing, not leave her wondering how she could have been so stupid.

'Jess?' he prompted.

'I thought you would leave me,' she said slowly.

'Like your father left your mother?'

'I was so young,' she whispered. 'You know I was.'

He looked at her and started speaking slowly, as if he was voicing his thoughts out loud. 'I'd like to tell you that my feelings haven't changed, but that would be strange, as well as a fabrication—because of course I feel differently eight years down the line.'

Her lips had started trembling and no amount of biting would seem to stop them. 'You do?'

He nodded. 'I still care about you, *koukla mou*. You're still the one woman who makes my heart beat faster than anyone else. Still the one who can tie me up in knots so tight I can't escape, and I don't think you even realise you're doing it.'

'So what are you saying?' she whispered.

Loukas opened his lips to speak, but an in-built self-protection forced him to temper his words with caution. Just like when you were negotiating a big takeover—you didn't lay all your cards on the table at once, did you? You always kept something back.

'I'm saying that it still feels…*unfinished*. That maybe we should give it another go. What's stopping us?'

She put her mug down and pulled the scrunchy from her hair, shaking her head so that a tumble of hair fell loosely around her cheeks.

'Loads of things. We live in different worlds, for a start,' she said. 'We always did, but it's even more defined now. I'm a country girl with a simple life. The annual photo shoot in London was just something I did to finance this life. The rest of the time, I forget all about it.'

'I'm not forcing you to become the global face of Lulu if you don't want to be,' he said impatiently. 'That's not what this is all about.'

'You're missing my point, Loukas,' she said, and now she was gesturing to something he hadn't noticed before, which lay on a small table in the corner of the room. A piece of cloth covered with exquisite sewing. He narrowed his eyes. It looked like a cosmic sky, with bright planets and stars sparking across an indigo background.

'Yours?' he questioned.

She nodded. 'Mine.'

'It's beautiful,' he said automatically.

'Thank you. It's something that's become more than a hobby and I've sold several pieces through a shop in Padstow. I'm into embroidery and gardening and now that Hannah's gone away, I was even thinking of getting a cat—that's how sad I am. You, on the other hand, live permanently in a hotel and drive around in a chauffeur-driven car. You occupy a luxury suite in the centre of London and you get other people to run your life for you. We're polar opposites, Loukas. You don't have a real home. You don't seem to want one and I do. That's what I want more than anything.' Her voice trembled, as if it hurt her to say the words. 'A real home.'

CHAPTER TWELVE

LOUKAS DIDN'T ANSWER straight away. It was
easier to watch the Atlantic crashing on the
rocks in the distance and to listen to the
crackle of the fire, rather than having to face
up to what Jess had just told him. He'd never
heard her be so frank and realised it must have
taken a lot for her to put her feelings on the
line like that. And even though he was determined to hold something back, that didn't
mean he couldn't proceed with caution, did it?

'What if I told you that the reason I don't
have a home is because I don't know how it
works?' he said. 'And that I've never been
sufficiently interested in the concept to find
out?'

'Well, there you go. You've answered your
own question.'

'But you could show me,' he continued, as
if she hadn't interrupted.

She stared at him and there was a mutinous look in her eyes as if she didn't believe him. As if she was waiting for him to pull out the punchline and start laughing. But he wasn't laughing, he was deadly serious and maybe she picked up on that. 'Because I don't feel this thing we have between us has run its course,' he said.

'This *thing*?'

'Don't get hung up on words, Jess.' His voice deepened. 'I'm Greek, remember?'

'As if I'm likely to forget.' She tucked a strand of hair behind her ear. 'And I don't really understand what you're suggesting.'

He shrugged. 'That I move in here with you and see whether I'm compatible with home life.'

She laughed. 'But you're an international playboy.'

He gave her a slow smile. 'That could be negotiable.'

'And you have a job.'

'I also have a computer and a phone—and the ability to pull back and delegate.' He looked at her steadily. 'And it's been a very long time since I had a vacation.'

Jessica stared down at her fingernails, her

initial disbelief at his suggestion morphing into a feeling of confusion. She suspected he was motivated more by ambition than any real emotion. He'd said himself this *thing* felt *unfinished* and maybe that was bugging him—because he was the kind of man who didn't like to leave things unfinished. Maybe this was all about great sex and the fact that they were still so attracted to one another. Was he banking on that attraction burning itself out, so that he could walk away? Just using the lure of *home* as a legitimate way to get his foot in the door?

Yet if he left now, what then? Would she spend the rest of her life regretting it and wondering *what if*? Too scared to face up to something which had lain beneath the surface of her life for so long, something which subconsciously might have been holding her back. There had been many times she'd wished she had the chance to do it all over again and now the opportunity was presenting itself. By allowing him access to her life, mightn't the pedestal she'd placed him on begin to crumble, freeing her from his power over her?

'If I said yes,' she said slowly, 'it could end at any time.'

'I can't guarantee—'

'No, Loukas.' She cut him off with a shake of her head, embarrassed that he thought she was trying to back him into a corner. 'I'm not asking you to pledge anything or promise anything. I'm trying to be practical because I'm a practical person.' She drew in a deep breath. 'If either of us wants out, at any time—any time at all—then we have to be able to say so. No questions. No post-mortems. Just a shrug and a smile, and a simple goodbye.'

His dark eyes gleamed. 'This is beginning to sound like my dream scenario.'

'I aim to please,' she said lightly.

He stood up and walked across the room and Jessica could almost *feel* the testosterone radiating from his powerful body.

'You certainly do. You please me very much.' His voice dipped. 'But if this is such an equal and such a *practical* arrangement, then surely I get to make a few requests myself, *koukla mou.*'

Something in the darkness of his face made her throat turn to parchment. 'Like what?' she questioned breathlessly.

'We may be playing house, but we aren't going to be constrained by house rules. We don't clock in and clock out. You won't start slamming cupboards if I'm late for dinner.'

'But you might be the one cooking dinner, and I might be the one who's late.'

'I might.' His eyes glittered. 'Just so long as you don't try to change me,' he said as his gaze travelled slowly over her body and seemed to linger there. 'And no rules about sex, either. We don't use it as a weapon or as a negotiating tool.'

'Gosh. You sound as if you've had some pretty bad experiences with women.'

'You think so?' He gave a cynical smile. 'I'd say it was the normal experience of a wealthy and attractive man who happens to be good in bed. And before you start pulling faces like that—I'm trying to be honest.' He paused. 'But again, in the pursuit of fairness—perhaps I should ask you the same thing. Have you had bad experiences with men?'

She hadn't been expecting the question and therefore hadn't prepared an answer, but now was not the time to make the announcement that there hadn't *been* anyone except for him. Apart from making her look hopelessly out of touch, mightn't it also make him wary? He might realise that nobody else had come close to making her feel the way he had done. That she had fallen for him big time. That she was expecting a whole lot more than he could ever give.

So she smiled. 'I thought we were going to have fun,' she said. 'Not rake up stuff about the past. The past has gone, Loukas, and this is what we're left with.'

'So it is.' He pulled her to her feet, tipping her chin upwards so that there was nowhere to look except at him, and when he spoke again his voice had deepened and suddenly it no longer sounded steady. 'I want you, Jess.'

'Let's go upstairs to bed,' she whispered.

He shook his head. 'I don't want to go anywhere. Draw the curtains.'

Her hands were trembling as she did as he asked, turning back to see his face looking shadowed in the suddenly subdued lighting broken only by the dancing flicker of the fire.

'Loukas,' she said uncertainly, and suddenly he was all over her. His hands were fumbling with the zip of her jeans, yanking them down to her ankles before impatiently tugging them off and hurling them to one side. He was peeling her sweater over her head and she was urging him on—silently positioning her body to make access easier. She shrugged the leather jacket from his broad shoulders and heard it slide to the floor. She eased the zip of his jeans down, but he was so aroused—the hard ridge of him so *big* beneath her still-trembling fingers —that he pushed her hand away.

'No. Let me,' he said succinctly, before freeing himself.

She gasped as he did so and it felt so deliciously decadent to be stripping off in the shadowy firelight that she reached down to cradle him in her hands but, again, he pushed her away—rapidly disposing of his own remaining clothes until they were both naked before the golden flicker of the flames.

'Now,' he said, but his voice sounded so tight and urgent that it was almost as if she had never heard him speak before. She was breathless and wet as he eased the condom on himself with an exaggerated amount of care, as if only by doing that could he hang onto a self-control which seemed perilously close to deserting him. And then he positioned himself over her, that first deep thrust making her moan and his subsequent rhythm making her moan ever more. Until he stopped and a mumbled protest fell from her lips.

'L-Loukas—'

'Open your eyes,' he ordered. 'Open your eyes and look at me.'

Reluctantly she let her lashes flutter apart to meet his smoky black gaze, afraid of what he might be able to read when all her defences were down. She tried to tell herself that this was what every woman felt when she was having sex with a man, but on some fundamental level she knew that wasn't true. Because surely it wasn't normal to feel as if your heart were on fire. As if you wanted to burst with joy. Those were the feelings you associated with love.

But Loukas wasn't looking for love. The reason he wanted her to open her eyes was to gauge her level of satisfaction, and there was no hiding *that*.

Her lashes flickered open completely, and he smiled.

'That's better,' he said. 'Tell me what you like, Jess. Tell me what you want me to do to you.'

She wondered what he expected—a verbal map to indicate just which zones she found most erogenous, or an expressed preference for a different position? But in reality, there was only one thing Jessica wanted Loukas to do to her.

'Just kiss me,' she said, because that was the closest she could get to asking him to love her.

CHAPTER THIRTEEN

BE CAREFUL WHAT you wish for.

Jessica stood at her bedroom window, watching Loukas in the garden below as he chopped logs and added them to the growing pile. It made for a compelling image. His strong arms swung in an arc as the blade splintered into the wood—drawing attention to the honed definition of muscles rippling across his shoulders and his broad back.

Her throat dried. How many times had she longed for a scenario like this, in those lonely moments when her fantasies about him wouldn't respond to censorship, no matter how hard she'd tried? She'd dreamed of Loukas being back in her life and in her bed—with the freedom to conduct their relationship openly in a way which had never been possible before. And now she had it. No more moments of passion sandwiched in between the strictures of her career and the demands of his billionaire boss. Now *he* was the billionaire—although she no longer had a career, she thought wryly. Still. It should have been great. It should have been almost perfect.

So why the questions which still whirled around in her mind, which felt as if they had no real answers?

Ever since he'd moved into her Cornish cottage, they'd behaved like a couple. They'd done stuff. The normal stuff which other people did. They'd cooked dinner and shopped for food, and at first it had been disorientating to see Loukas in the local store, standing among all the villagers and the occasional tourist. People stopped what they were doing and turned to look at him and it was easy to see why. With his leather jacket and faded jeans, he looked larger than life—tall and indomitable. A dark, head-turning presence who seemed to come from a very different world.

Because he had. That was exactly what he had done. He'd known violence, rejection, pain and despair and those things had given him an edge which marked him out from other men. No wonder everyone else had always seemed so pale and so tame in comparison. No wonder no other man had ever been able to coax her into his bed.

Very quickly Jessica discovered that she liked having him around. She liked being part of a couple and doing coupley things. It made life more interesting to have a man to watch a scary film with, and play the old-fashioned board games which she taught him and which he was soon winning. She liked the feel of his warm, naked body when she got into bed at night and his arms wrapped around her waist when she woke up in the morning. She liked knowing they could make love whenever and wherever they liked.

But she was also aware of the subtle boundaries which surrounded them. The unspoken, instinctive restrictions. They never talked about the future and they never used the word love. He might have seamlessly slotted into having a home, but it still felt like *her* home, not his. As if he had invested nothing in it, nor was he planning to. Of course he hadn't. Because, when she stopped to think about it for long enough, could she really imagine Loukas Sarantos living the rest of his life in some rural Cornish outlet?

And despite his intention to delegate, his

other life soon began to snap around at his heels, like a puppy demanding to be played with. It started with the odd phone call here and there and the beginning of a mounting pile of emails which needed to be dealt with. Soon there were conference calls, which he told her he had to take.

Jessica usually absented herself for those. She would go out into the garden, hearing his deep voice drifting through the open window—often speaking Greek—while she stared down at the bare soil and wondered when the first daffodils would push through and show that spring was nearly here.

She had just straightened up from plucking a weed from the ground after one such call, when she felt the warm caress of Loukas's hand splaying over her denim-covered buttock and she gave a little shiver of pleasure.

She threw the weed onto the compost heap. 'Everything okay?'

'The conference call was fine. And then my brother rang.' There was a pause. 'My twin.'

Jessica turned around, hearing his deliberate emphasis of the word and knowing just why he did that. She guessed it was still weird for him to acknowledge that he actually *had* a twin—

the amazingly successful Alek Sarantos. She knew that contact between the two men had been minimal, but maybe that wasn't so surprising, since neither had known about the other's existence until they were grown men.

'How is he?'

He shrugged. 'He's okay. Actually, he's in London.'

'Oh.' Wasn't it stupid that just the mention of the city sounded vaguely *ominous*, as if it posed some kind of threat? She felt as if his other world—the one she wasn't part of—was beginning to inch towards them. Her smile didn't slip. 'That's nice.'

'Mmm. He wants me to have dinner with him. I thought I'd stay up for a few days. Do a little work while I'm there.' He narrowed his black eyes. 'You could always come with me.'

She lifted her hand to his face, her fingertips drifting over the sculptured outline of his unshaven jaw and feeling its rough rasp. Yes, she could. She could accompany him to London, a trip which would require a frantic mental inventory about what to wear. She could gatecrash his meeting with his newfound brother and inhibit their burgeoning relationship. She could hang around the Vinoly while he went into the office, or dutifully kill hours doing cultural things with which to impress him when he got home.

She got a sudden scary glimpse of how the future might look, once the initial wild sexual excitement had started to fade. He would probably start making more trips to London and each time he came back, it would be a little harder for them to reconnect. That was how these things worked, wasn't it? How long before he told her he was moving back permanently to the city, to the rented hotel suite he called home? Deep-down she knew she didn't fit into his life in London and that was his base.

So shouldn't she start getting used to that—with pride and with dignity?

'You need some time on your own with Alek,' she said. 'I'll stay here.'

His mouth tightened. 'Right.'

She saw the sudden flinty look in his eyes. Did it matter to him if she accompanied him or not?

So ask him. Just go right ahead and ask him.

But the different ways of phrasing such a question were really only a disguise for the one which could never be asked.

How do you feel about me, Loukas?

A more confident woman might have come right out and said it. A more sexually experienced one almost certainly would have done. But Jessica had been protecting herself from pain for so long that she would sooner have walked barefoot across the rough cliff path than risk getting hurt again.

'When will you leave?' she said as they began to walk back towards the house.

'I'll leave immediately. Why hang around? There's just one thing I need to do first.'

She turned her face up to look at him. 'What's that?'

'I'll show you.'

He linked his fingers with hers and led her inside, taking her straight upstairs and stripping off her clothes with speed rather than finesse. His eyes were still flinty and his mouth hardened into an odd kind of smile just before he drove it down on hers in a punishing kind of kiss.

He entered her urgently and as Jessica clung to his thrusting body she was filled with a terrible sense of *sadness*—as if she'd just failed a test she hadn't even known she was taking.

The house was quiet after he'd left. It was

the first time she'd been without him for weeks. Long, lazy weeks which now seemed to have passed in a flash. She kept looking up, expecting to see him, telling herself it was crazy how quickly she had become used to having him around.

She kept busy, working hard on her embroidery and selling a small piece privately, before hearing about the possibility of a commission for a much larger piece. She gardened and made bread and went for long cliff-top walks. Then she took a call from an excited Hannah, who told her that she'd met a young Australian vet in Bali.

'Oh, Jess,' she sighed. 'He's gorgeous. You'd really like him. He wants me to go to Perth next. That's where his folks live.'

'That sounds lovely,' said Jessica, even though inside she wanted to scream, *Please don't fall in love with a man from the other side of the world, so that I probably won't see you very much.*

Because you shouldn't use your own selfish needs to try to change someone else's behaviour, should you? Wasn't that one of the reasons why she never dared bring up the subject of the future with Loukas—because she sensed there could never be any compromise about their different lifestyles? Or because she wasn't sure if his feelings for her went any deeper than a powerful sexual attraction? She thought about him, miles away in London, and her heart clenched. Did he miss her, she wondered, and did he have any idea how much she missed him?

She spoke to him that evening and the sound of laughter and glasses clinking in the background made her feel very alone. And it was her own stupid fault. She thought that if he'd suggested her joining him, she would have been booking her ticket from Bodmin station quicker than a flash. But he didn't. Just as he didn't know *exactly* when he would be back.

'Soon,' he said.

But *soon* was inconclusive. *Soon* gave her the chance to dwell on all the things which were nagging away inside her. Maybe his brother was lining him up with a nice Greek girl. Maybe the lure of London had enticed him back and the thought of returning to this quiet little hamlet had filled him with horror.

Or just maybe he was missing her as much as she was missing him. What if that was a possibility? And once she allowed herself to consider *that* possibility, it altered everything. It scared her. It excited her. It made her feel as if she were floating three inches about the ground. She thought about some of the things he'd told her. About a mother who had always put other men before her son. Didn't that mean he would be reluctant to trust the love of women—or wary about putting his own feelings on the line? So wasn't it time to start grabbing at a little emotional courage— to dare show Loukas that she wanted him? To stop worrying about the fear of rejection and tell him she cared.

A text arrived from him in the early hours and she stared at it sleepily.

Back tomorrow. ☹ xxx

She woke, still with that walking-on-air feeling. She cleaned the house from top to bottom and swept the path. At the village store, she bought coffee, bread and wine—and when she got home went out into the garden, snipping off bright stems of foliage to cram into a beautiful blue and white vase. When he arrived she would tell him she'd missed him. Or ask him whether he wanted her to return to

London with him. Because home was where you made it, wasn't it? She might not particularly like London, but wouldn't she rather live there with him than live in the countryside without him? Couldn't she show him that she could be adaptable?

She'd just washed the mud from her hands when the phone started ringing and eagerly she snatched it up, surprised but pleased to hear Patti, the spiky-haired stylist from Zeitgeist, on the end of the line and remembering the conversation they'd had at the launch party.

'If you're ringing about meeting for coffee, then it'll have to wait,' said Jessica. 'I'm in Cornwall.'

'Oh, okay.' There was a pause. 'Jessica...this might sound like a crazy question but I don't suppose Loukas is with you, is he?'

Afterwards, Jessica would think how strange the human brain was—that it could sift out a single word from a sentence and focus on that alone.

'Why would it be crazy?' she asked, because maybe it was time to stop pretending this wasn't happening. To start acknowledging that she and Loukas were in some sort of *relationship*.

'Oh, just that someone at Lulu said they thought you two were dating.'

'I don't know that I'd exactly describe it as dating. But, well, yes. He's been staying here.'

'So it worked,' said Patti, in a flat kind of voice.

'What worked?'

'It doesn't matter.'

'Oh, come on, Patti—you can't do that. You can't half say something and then leave me wondering the worst.'

There was a pause. 'I like you, Jessica. I like you very much.'

'And I like you, too. Mutual admiration society established. So what aren't you telling me?'

Another pause. 'Remember when the photos weren't working that first time in Venice? You know—when you were all wooden in front of the camera.'

'Yes, I remember. What about it?'

Patti's voice sounded hesitant. 'It's just that the art director said that what they really needed was for you to look like a woman who had just had sex. And the next day you did. The photos were absolute dynamite and everyone thought...'

'Everyone thought, what—that Loukas had taken the suggestion literally?'

'Something like that,' said Patti uncomfortably. 'And I wouldn't say anything, but… Well, it's just that he has such a reputation, and I'd hate to see you getting hurt. I'm sorry. Maybe I shouldn't have said anything.'

'No,' said Jessica, with soft urgency. 'You should. Don't worry about it, Patti. You did exactly the right thing. You told me something I needed to know.'

She couldn't settle to anything after that. Loukas rang to say he was on his way back and she slumped down into the chair, her embroidery untouched and nothing really registering until she saw the low flash of winter sun glinting from his windscreen.

Her heart had started pounding and her palms were clammy. Wiping them down over her jeans, she prepared to greet him. And even while her heart was feeling the pain, she was running the whole scene like a film through her mind. This is the last time I'll see him drive up here like this, she thought. The last time he'll walk up this little path with the sun glinting off his black hair. The last, dying moments of being a couple were almost upon her and Jessica could barely summon up a smile with which to greet him.

But she didn't want this to turn into some kind of awful screaming match. She'd witnessed enough of those before her parents' divorce to put her off displays of high emotion for ever. She would be very calm and very dignified. It might even come as something of a relief to Loukas. For all she knew, he might have been trying to work out a diplomatic way of ending it himself. She wasn't going to do accusations, or regret. She would do it neatly and without a scene, just as she'd promised right at the beginning.

His sleek car came to a halt and he got out. She saw those impossibly long legs unfolding themselves and the expression on that dark and rugged face making her feel...

She gave herself a mental shake. She wasn't going to *feel* anything. It was safer that way.

The crunch of the gravel was replaced by the sound of a door being opened and closed and then suddenly he was standing in front of her, framed in the doorway, like some dark and golden statue come to life.

'Hello, Loukas,' she said.

'Hello, Jess.'

Loukas waited for her to jump out of the chair and fling her arms around him. But she didn't. She just sat there in her jeans and sweater staring up at him, with those extraordinary aquamarine eyes narrowed and giving nothing away.

She never gave anything away, did she?

'Did you have a good trip?'

'Good in parts,' he said, just about to tell her that he'd missed her when something stopped him, only he wasn't sure what. He stared into her tense face. Perhaps he was starting to get a good idea.

He looked around the room, noticing the spray of berried branches in a blue and white vase and he narrowed his eyes in surprise, because that wasn't usually the kind of detail he noticed.

'So how was your brother?'

'Is my brother the reason you're sitting there looking so uptight?' he questioned. 'Is my brother the reason you haven't kissed me, or looked as if you're pleased to see me?'

'I'm very pleased to see you.'

'Liar,' he said softly. 'Or maybe you're just not as good at hiding your feelings as you used to be. Are you going to tell me what's bugging you, Jess—or are we going to play a game of elimination?'

She shook her head as if she was having some kind of silent tussle with herself and when she spoke, it was as if she was picking her words with care.

'Let me ask *you* a question, Loukas. How important was it to turn the company around, when you bought Lulu?'

He shrugged. 'Very important—naturally. I'm a businessman and success is part of the deal—the biggest and most measurable part there is.'

She nodded as if his answer had just reinforced something she already knew, and suddenly her hands were clenching into fists so tight he could see the whitening of her knuckles.

'Did you have sex with me just to get me to relax for the photo shoot?' she hissed.

'What?'

'You heard me perfectly well. Don't try to think up a clever answer—just tell me the truth.'

'You seem to have already decided for yourself what the truth is, without bothering to reference me first,' he snapped. 'Where the hell has all this come from?'

'It doesn't matter where it came from. Just that I heard that after the first disastrous shoot in Venice, the art director said I needed to look as if I'd just had sex.' Her cheeks were flushed and her eyes defiant as she stared him full in the face. 'And so...'

Her words tailed off and he felt his heart clench with anger. 'And so you thought that I would make the ultimate sacrifice for the sake of the company? That I'd take you to bed and loosen you up, thus ensuring that we had the requisite sultry photos to headline the new campaign. Is that what you thought, Jess?'

She opened her mouth and then closed it again, before nodding her head so vigorously that her blonde hair shimmered up and down.

'Yes,' she said fervently. 'That's exactly what I thought because it's the truth, isn't it, Loukas?'

He stared at her for a long moment and then he began to laugh.

CHAPTER FOURTEEN

FEELING WRONG-FOOTED, Jessica stared into Loukas's face—wondering how he had the *nerve* to laugh at a moment like this.

'What's so funny?' she demanded.

Only now the smile had gone. It had died on his lips, leaving nothing in its place but a look of withering contempt.

'You are,' he said. 'You're priceless. Do you really think that I would have cold-bloodedly had sex with you, just to make a better photo? I've heard of naked ambition, but really! Just how far do you think my dedication to the company goes, Jess? Do you think I would have done the same if I'd only just met the model, or found her physically repulsive? That I'd be acting like some kind of male whore?'

She glared at him. How dared he try to turn this round? 'You were talking to loads of different women at the party!' she accused.

'You know you were. Just not to me. But then, you've been hiding me away like a dirty secret, haven't you? You acted like you barely knew me at the party. Like we were strangers!'

He frowned. 'Because I didn't think either of us were ready to go public right then. And yes, I was talking to other women there—but it doesn't automatically follow that I was planning on having sex with them.'

Her eyes bored into his. 'Not even Maya?' she accused.

'Maya?' he echoed blankly, until his face cleared. 'Oh, Maya. You mean my ex-lover? Why, would you have had me blank her and be rude to her by ignoring her? That isn't the kind of behaviour I'd expect from a classy lady like you, Jess.'

His sarcasm washed over her and she glared at him. 'You hired me for all kinds of reasons,' she bit out. 'But I got the distinct impression that the main one was because you wanted to get even with me. That you'd never quite forgiven me for everything that happened before. And please don't try and make out I'm a fool, Loukas—or that I imagined it. You did. You know you did.'

There was a pause before he answered and

then he sucked in a breath and nodded his head slowly. 'At the beginning, maybe I did,' he said. 'But things change, Jess—only you seem to be blind to them. You only ever see the shallow stuff—you never dare scratch beneath the surface, do you? When we reconnected again after all those years I agree that initially I felt a mixture of anger and lust. And if you really want the truth, I thought that getting you out of my system was going to be simple.'

'By sleeping with me?' she demanded.

'*Neh*. By sleeping with you.' He gave a cynical laugh. 'Actually, sleeping had nothing to do with it. I wanted you wide awake and very present. I wanted to do something that I'd been unable to forget and that was to have sex with you again. But you fought me all the way. You didn't just fall into my arms, even though I knew you wanted to. You forced me to get to know you again and to realise—'

'Realise what?'

'It doesn't matter.' He shook his head and his voice had grown cold now—as cold as the icy glint from his eyes. 'None of it does. Doesn't matter that I indulged you—'

'*Indulged me?*'

'*Neh*. I treated you with kid gloves,' he

gritted out. 'I was cautious and careful. I put my business on hold and came to live with you here because I know you don't like London, but it still wasn't enough, was it? Because nothing is ever enough for you, Jess. You couldn't wait to think the worst of me—to give you a reason not to trust me. A reason to send me away and lock yourself away again—with all your beauty and your warmth hidden behind the frozen front you present to the world.'

'Loukas—'

'No!' he flared impatiently. 'I don't intend to spend my life tiptoeing around you, while you imagine the worst. Believe what you want to believe, because I'm done with this. And I'm done with you.'

His tone was harsh and Jessica stared at him, wondering what he was doing, then realised he was tugging his car keys from the pocket of his jacket and preparing to leave.

He was preparing to leave, only this time the look on his face told her he would never come back.

'Loukas,' she said again, fingertips flying to her mouth in horror. But her gasped word didn't stop him or make his stony face relax.

He was opening the front door and the chill March wind was whistling through the door as he walked out, sending the temperature plummeting.

Frozen, he'd called her, and she *felt* frozen. Frozen enough to feel as if she were encased in ice when she heard a door slam and the sound of an engine firing into life. She turned her head to see the car bumping over the grass onto the unmade road, with Loukas's stony profile staring straight ahead.

He was going.

He was going.

'Loukas!' She ran outside and the cry was torn from her throat as she screamed it into the wind, but if he heard her, he didn't stop. And if he saw her that made no difference either, because the car continued to move forward. Waving her arms in the air, she started to run after it. To run as she hadn't run in years. It was like running across the court for a ball she knew she would never reach, only…

The last time that had happened she had ruptured her cruciate ligament and ended her career with a sickening snap, but this time she couldn't move as fast as her teenage self and her footsteps slowed to a stumbled halt. This time all that she had ruptured was her heart, yet somehow the pain seemed just as intense.

Sinking to her knees on the damp ground, she buried her face in her hands and began to cry, great sobs welling up from somewhere deep inside her chest until they erupted into a raw howl of pain. She wept at her own stupidity and timidity—at her lack of courage at going after something she realised now was irreplaceable. She could have had him—the only man she had ever cared about—but she'd been too proud and too stupid and too scared to give it a go. Too afraid of being hurt to take a risk, when everyone knew that love never came without some element of risk.

Hot tears dripped through her frozen fingers, drying instantly in the chill wind, and as she began to shiver she knew she couldn't stay there for ever. Her teeth chattering, she rose slowly to her feet, blinking away tears as she stared into the distance and saw the dark shape of a distinctive car parked on the clifftop and her heart missed a beat.

Loukas's car.

She blinked again as she realised that her eyes weren't playing tricks on her, but that it was definitely *his* car and he hadn't gone.

He hadn't gone.

With stumbling steps she began to run—expecting at any moment to see it disappear into the distance in a swift acceleration of power. But it didn't and her stride became longer—her panting breath making clouds of vapour in the chill air as she began to make silent pleas in her head. *Please don't go. Please just give me one more chance and I'll never let you down again.*

Out of breath, she reached the car at last. He was sitting perfectly still, staring straight ahead until she began to rap on the window and then he turned his head to look at her. His black eyes were flinty and his dark features were unreadable, but these days such a look was rare. She remembered the night when she'd been exhausted and wrung out in Venice. When he'd put her to bed and fed her melted cheese. When he'd made her feel safe and cherished as well as desired, and her heart swelled with an immense feeling of love and longing.

'Don't go,' she mouthed, through the glass. 'Please.'

He didn't say a word as he took the key from the ignition and climbed out of the car.

He stared down at her for a long moment and then the flicker of a smile appeared on his lips.

'I wasn't,' he said, 'planning on going anywhere. I just needed time to cool down, before I said something I might afterwards regret.'

'Oh, Loukas,' she said, her words still muffled from all the crying she'd done.

But as Loukas looked at her he knew it had been more than that. He'd wanted to see if she would come after him, and she had. He'd wanted to show her that he had staying power. He needed her to know that she could trust him, because without that there could be no real love. And he knew he really couldn't hold back any longer.

'Because what I really want to say is that I love you, Jess,' he said simply. 'I love you. Completely, absolutely and enduringly.'

'Oh, Loukas,' she said as she flung her arms around his neck and pressed her cold face to his. 'I feel exactly the same about you. I love you so much, and I've made such a mess of showing you.'

'Then show me,' he said fiercely. 'Show me now.' And when she lifted her face to his, her eyes were very bright as he brushed his lips over hers.

The kiss deepened. He kissed her until they were both breathless and when he pulled away they were smiling—as if they'd just allowed themselves to see something which had been there all the time. He put her into the car and snapped her seat belt closed and when he'd parked outside her cottage, he took her hand and led her inside. He made coffee and smoothed the hair from her eyes and it was only when she was sitting snuggled up against him on the sofa that he looked down at her gravely.

'But there are a few things we need to get cleared up before we go any further.'

'Mmm?' she said dreamily, her head resting against his shoulder.

'Just for the record—I know you aren't a city girl,' he said. 'And you don't have to be, because all I want to do is to marry you and make a home with you. Where that home will be is entirely up to you.'

'Loukas—'

'No, Jess,' he said. 'Hear me out. I need you to know that I'm not saying any of this in reaction to what has just happened. I need you to know that I've been thinking about this and have wanted it for a long while.'

She opened her eyes wide. 'You have?'

'I have. When I was in London I talked to my brother about it, in a way I've never talked to anyone.' He smiled. 'Except maybe you. I told him that I was in love with you but that I thought you were scared because you kept pushing me away every time I tried to get closer.'

She sniffed again. 'And what did he say?'

'He said that deep down most people are scared of love, because they recognise it has the power to hurt them like nothing else can. And that there are no guarantees in life.'

'You mean that nothing is certain?'

'Absolutely nothing,' he agreed, and now she could see the pain in his own eyes. 'But we both know how important it is to succeed at this. We've both had things happen which make it hard for us to believe it ever can, but I know it can. I think we both want this relationship to work more than we've ever wanted trophies, or money in the bank, or houses and cars.' His voice deepened. 'I know I do.'

'So do I,' she said in a squeaky voice which sounded perilously close to more tears.

'Because at the end of the day, love is the only thing which matters, and it is important that we mark that love.' He reached into his pocket and pulled out a familiarly coloured magenta box, tied with the distinctive Lulu ribbon. 'Which is why I want to ask you to be my wife.'

She swallowed. 'You've already bought me a ring?'

His face was grave. 'Well, I had the choice of some of the world's finest jewels.'

He flipped open the box and Jessica blinked. She had been expecting to be dazzled by diamonds, but all that lay on the indigo velvet was a small, metal ring-pull—the type you found on a can of cola.

She looked at him in surprise, with the first flicker of amusement tugging at her lips. 'And this is my engagement ring?'

He shrugged. 'Everything seemed such a cliché. Aquamarine to match your eyes, or diamonds for their cold and glittering beauty? With a whole empire at my disposal I was spoilt for choice—and I gather that, these days, the trend is to let women choose what they really, really want.'

'Put it on,' she said fiercely, and as he slid the worthless piece of metal onto her finger she saw that it was trembling. And she thought that being with Loukas Sarantos made a mockery of the steady hands which had once been her trademark. But she was smiling as she cupped his face in her hands and pressed her own very close.

'I don't want your diamonds,' she whispered. 'You're the only thing I really, really want. Your love and your commitment. They are more precious to me than all the jewels in the world, and I will treasure them and keep them close to my heart. Because I want you to know that I love you, Loukas Sarantos. I always have and I always will. A diamond isn't for ever. Love is.'

EPILOGUE

'HAPPY?' LOUKAS NUZZLED his mouth over Jess's bare shoulder and felt her wriggle luxuriously.

Turning her head towards his, she smiled.

'Totally,' she sighed.

'Sure?'

'How could I not be?' She traced his mouth with a tender finger. 'You're my husband and I'm your wife. Your pregnant wife.'

He saw the way that her eyes flashed with joy and that pleased him. It pleased him that he could read her so well—and that these days she was happy to let him. And he recognised you couldn't change the past overnight. You had to work at things. No pain—no gain.

And yet the gain.

Ah, the gain.

He sighed with contentment as he stared out of the window, where the massive Greek sun was beginning its scarlet and vibrant ascendancy. The most dazzling sunrises he'd ever seen had been here, on the island where he'd been born and then taken away from as a wriggling baby, too young to remember its powdery white sands or the crystal seas after which it had been named.

Until now.

Kristalothos was one of the most beautiful places he'd ever seen, although he'd been reluctant to return at first, because it symbolised a dark time of his life. But Jess had gently persuaded him that it would be healthy to lay this particular ghost to rest.

His first trip back had been with his twin, Alek—just the two of them, when they'd stood and stared at the luxury hotel which had replaced the fortress in which Alek had grown up. It had been razed to the ground and now, as a luxury hotel, it was a place of light, not shade. And the two brothers had swum and fished, and listened to the night herons as they'd gathered around the lapping bay. And they'd talked. They'd talked long into the night, having conversations which had been over thirty years in the making.

Loukas had gone home to Jess and told her

that the island was a paradise and when she'd suggested spending part of their honeymoon there during their tour of the Greek islands, he had readily agreed. He wanted to show her the place of his birth and to share it with her. He wanted to share pretty much everything with her.

He looked at the platinum and diamond wedding band which gleamed on her finger. It had been the most amazing wedding—especially for a man who didn't like weddings. But he had liked his own. He had liked making those solemn vows and declaring to the world that Jessica Cartwright was his. She had always been his, and she would remain so for as long as he drew breath.

Hannah had been their bridesmaid—resplendent in a blue silk dress which had contrasted with her gap year tan—overjoyed to have the big brother she'd always longed for.

Alek had been his best man and his wife, Ellie, Jess's matron of honour. And their young son, named Loukas after his uncle, had been the cute hit of the day as he had toddled down the aisle as pageboy behind the bride.

One of the first things Loukas had done was to terminate the contract on his suite at the

Vinoly. He had told Jess he was prepared to work as much as possible from the west of the country, if she really wanted to stay there. But Jess had changed, just as much as he had. She hadn't wanted to be apart from him for a second longer than she needed to be, and she'd agreed to live in London, just so long as they had a garden.

So now they were in Hampstead, with not only their own garden, but a huge heath nearby, on which they would soon be able to take their son or daughter in a big, old-fashioned pram.

'Are you?'

Her soft voice broke into his thoughts and he stirred lazily as he met her questioning look. 'Am I what?'

'Happy.'

He smiled as he placed a hand over her still-flat belly and looked up into her shining eyes. 'I love you, Jess Sarantos,' he said. 'I love you more than I ever thought I could love anyone and you're now my wife. Does that answer your question?'

'It does,' she murmured and gave a contented little wriggle as he continued to stroke her belly with that same seductive, circular movement. She closed her eyes. 'Mmm. That's nice. Any ideas about what you'd like to do today?'

'More of the same,' he said, his husky words made indistinct by the lazy pressure of his kiss. 'Just more of the same.'

* * * * *

LARGER-PRINT BOOKS!

GET 2 FREE LARGER-PRINT NOVELS PLUS
2 FREE GIFTS!

◊ **HARLEQUIN**®

Romance

From the Heart, For the Heart

HRLP15

LARGER-PRINT BOOKS!
GET 2 FREE LARGER-PRINT NOVELS PLUS
2 FREE GIFTS!

H HARLEQUIN®

super romance

More Story...More Romance